MW01137169

Other Titles by Veryl Ann Grace

Murder Spins a Tale

Murder Comes Unraveled

A Flock and Fiber Mystery

Veryl Ann Grace

Pele's Hair Publishing

This is a work of fiction. Any names, characters, businesses, organizations, places or events are either the product of the author's imagination or used fictitiously.

Copyright © 2012 Veryl Ann Grace

Cover Art: Charlene Lofgreen
Interior Art: Kary Miksis
Author photo: Glenn Grace
Interior Book Design: Linda M. Au

All rights reserved. No part of this book may be reproduced in any form or by any means, including photocopying and recording, or by any information storage and retrieval system, electronic or mechanical, except for brief passages quoted in a review without the written permission of the author.

For more information, contact:
Pele's Hair Publishing
PO Box 1330
Kea`au, Hawai`i 96749

ISBN-13: 978-1-4791-0067-5
ISBN-10: 1-4791-0067-6

In Memory of

Linda M Weisser
Mentor, Beloved Friend, and
Great Pyrenees Breeder Extraordinaire

Acknowledgments

First and foremost, I want to thank all the readers of *Murder Spins a Tale*. Your delight in Martha, Denali and Falcor's story has been exciting and wonderful. I feel like I have made new friends all around the world. Here is the second book you requested. It is for you that we tell the stories.

One of the challenges for an author is coming up with a unique title. Lara Toomey Smoot suggested *Murder Comes Unraveled* and won a small contest on my blog. Thanks, Lara.

Thanks as well to Alicia Santiago of Arizona Llama Rescue, who helped me keep my facts straight when it came to camelid behavior and care. Any errors are mine, not hers.

Thank you to Helen Fleischer and Barrie Eskridge for your great job of beta reading. The story improved with your help.

Thanks to the Productive Spinners Yahoo Group that let me once again list a project that had little or nothing to do with spinning. You and Talia helped keep me on track and your support helped all along the way.

Many thanks to my production team who give you a book that is beautiful to look at: Linda M Au, who does my final proofreading and book design; Charlene Lofgreen for the beautiful cover art; and Kary Miksis for the interior art. You can find out more about Linda's work on her Facebook page, Author Linda M Au; Charlene's work is viewable at www.ArtWanted. com/clofgreen; and Kary can be found on Facebook under The Knotty Sheep.

As always, hugs go to Judy Gustafson for all of her support no matter what crazy thing I decide to do this time.

And to my husband, Glenn, thanks for ignoring me when I'm deep into my stories and don't want to be bothered. Love you.

You can connect with me on the web at www.verylanngrace. com and at my blogs http:/flocknfibermysteries.blogspot.com and http://fiberinparadise.blogspot.com You will also find me on Facebook and Twitter. Both accounts are under my name— Veryl Ann Grace. Hope to meet you out there.

Chapter 1

A large red-tailed hawk banked and let out a scream as it took after a smaller crow. White fluffy clouds were floating across the sky; it was a glorious May afternoon. I could see billows of dust ahead of me as another pickup with a trailer turned into the parking lot of the Black Hills Riding Academy. I was close behind, and as I pulled in beside it, Dorothy Swanson, a sheep rancher and the mother of my friend and attorney, David Swanson, climbed out of the cab.

"Hi, Dorothy. Are you selling flock or fiber?" I asked.

"Both," she answered. "I have some lambs for sale and a number of fleeces. One is a particularly nice Corriedale that you might like. Be sure and check it out."

"Sounds good. I'll do that when they open the fleece sale. Right now, I need to find out where they have located my booth and what stalls I have for the alpaca."

I turned and started walking toward the Academy Arena.

A huge wooden building, it was usually used for riding lessons, horse shows and junior rodeos. However, for the next four days it would be home to the Black Hills Fiber Gathering. The Gathering was an annual festival celebrating flocks and the fiber that came from them. Ranchers would be selling their animals and the fleece they produced. Other vendors would be selling anything and everything that could be connected, however vaguely, to the Gathering.

It was a weekend I always looked forward to. There was the air of a county fair but with the emphasis totally on the things that I liked best about a fair—fiber and fiber animals. There would be classes in a number of the fiber arts, some taught by nationally known teachers, and the fleece judging would bring out the best fleece that our local ranchers produced. Plus I would get a chance to spend the weekend with many people that I only saw at festivals like this one. It should be a great four days.

"You aren't selling Juan and Joseph, are you?" Dorothy asked as she walked beside me.

"No," I answered. "They're here as examples of the breed only. No one signed up to sell alpaca and Rex wanted some for exhibition. He knows my two are gentle and used to people, so he called me. I was a little reluctant to bring them as it's always stressful, but I hated to turn down Rex. He does a fine job of organizing the Black Hills Fiber Gathering and this is the first time that he's asked a favor of me."

"He does do an excellent job and you couldn't pay me to do it," Dorothy said. "There's always someone who's unhappy with his decisions and willing to make everyone's life miserable because of it."

She finished her sentence as we reached the large open doors of the arena. From the inside, we could hear angry voices.

"Looks like it's started already," I said.

"Well, I get to avoid it for now," she said with a grin. "My animals are in one of the out buildings this year. Rex had more people who wanted to sell than stalls in the main arena. I told him I wouldn't mind being put in one of the stables. I'm well aware that people wander among all the buildings during the Gathering, and it actually may be a little more peaceful for the animals."

In addition to the large arena, the academy property included four or five stables to house horses as well as some storage buildings and a covered area that had picnic tables in it when there were events happening.

"OK, I'll see you later then," I said as she turned to head toward the stable area. I continued to watch her as she walked quickly away. She had a long, purposeful stride that spoke of her time in the out-of-doors. The light breeze caught her short, gray curls and ruffled them, causing them to glint and shine in the afternoon sun. Sensing I was still by the door, she looked back and gave me a quick wave and a grin before she turned the corner.

With no excuse to stay outside any longer, I entered the big double doors of the arena and had to stop while my eyes adjusted to the dim interior. The floor of the main area was a packed rubber compound in a brick red color that covered most of the building. Above it on one side and at the ends were bleachers to allow spectators to view events happening in the arena. Along the other side, there were permanent horse stalls separated from the arena floor by a walkway and an eight-foot-high wall. For the Fiber Gathering, portable stalls were placed against that wall and throughout most of the arena floor area. Along the other wall below the bleachers, the vendors would set up their booths in two rows facing each other. Vending booth space was always at a premium, and often there was a waiting list to get in. It appeared, from what Dorothy said, that the same was true for animal stalls this year.

As I got further into the arena, the angry voices that Dorothy and I had heard outside once again caught my attention.

"What do you mean, you son of a bitch? I reserved six stalls and now you're telling me I only have four?"

I looked over to where the voices were and saw that Rex Meredith, the Gathering's organizer, and a large woman dressed in jeans and a plaid shirt were standing almost toe to toe. Neither one looked happy. Although the woman looked like she was close to my height of five feet seven inches, she was dwarfed by Rex's height, which was well over six feet; and it caused her to have to crane her neck to look up at him. I could see that her hands were balled up into fists and a few fringes of black hair had pulled away from the large braid atop her head. Her whole demeanor said she was angry enough to take a swing at the man if she'd thought she could get away with it.

"Catalin," Rex responded, "I have the paperwork you filled out here and it has you reserving four stalls. You reserved four stalls, and four stalls are what you have."

"I called you a month ago and left a message to add two additional stalls to that reservation. You didn't call me back and say I didn't have them so I have animals with me to fill six stalls. I can't take them back home. I'm here for the weekend, so you better find the additional two stalls for me. And pronto."

"I never got that message," Rex said; "and I have no stalls to spare. I even have two of the stables filled with animals. We're full up. You'll just have to double up somehow to use the four stalls that you have."

"I can't do that, you knucklehead. I have two rams with me who must have a stall each. And I have ten lambs and a ewe; I can't get them into two stalls. You've got to find me more room, and I want it now."

"Look," Rex said, "I have four stalls. That's all. I can't create them out of nothing."

I could hear the strain in his voice and was well aware that he was doing everything possible not to start screaming back at the woman.

"Well, then give me someone else's stall. I bet you have someone who could squeeze if you told them to."

"Now why would that be fair? You reserved four stalls; you have four stalls. Why should I take a stall from someone else?"

"I'm going to go to the founding committee if you don't. I'll let them know that you've singled me out because you're getting even. I'll make sure that everyone here knows what a jerk you are. You're bringing our personal dispute into the Gathering and using it as a way to get even with me."

"Listen, lady, and listen up good. Our dispute is being handled outside of this arena. I don't bring my personal business into the Fiber Gathering. I'm dealing with a limited number of stalls, and you have four. That's it, period, unless someone else gives one up. You figure it out."

Rex turned on his heel and stomped off. I could tell that he was distressed because his limp was more pronounced than usual. His left leg had been injured during the Vietnam War, leaving him with a slight limp that showed more when he was tired or under stress. The woman whirled around and came toward me so fast that she would have mowed me down if I hadn't moved aside. Instead she glared at me and gave a kick at a rock as she headed out into the parking lot.

I watched her for a minute, wondering who she was. I didn't remember seeing her at previous Gatherings. But then I hadn't been to that many of them. This was only my third, and at the first one, I didn't have my own booth. I was just here with the Great Pyrenees club.

My name is Martha Williamson and I own The Spider's Web, a fiber arts center where I offer supplies for and teach classes in spinning, weaving, knitting and crochet. Located on my property, it has become a gathering place for people who enjoy playing with yarn and allows me to make a living combining my love of fiber and teaching. I didn't start out as a small business owner, but life sometimes changes the path we're on.

Five years ago, the Air Force transferred my husband, John, and I from Hickam Air Force Base in Honolulu to McChord just outside of Tacoma, Washington. This was to be our last duty station, so when we were house shopping, we looked for a permanent home. We found it in a small twenty-five acre farm just outside of Black Hills, Washington. With its large farmhouse, wonderful old barn, and lovely garden, it was the perfect place for us: a spot of tranquility and peace after a busy day and often stressful commute to our jobs.

But that peace was shattered four years ago when John was killed on Halloween while driving to work on Interstate Five. A trucker fell asleep at the wheel and smashed John and his Toyota into the center barrier. I couldn't believe at the time that John, who had flown many hours in combat zones and arrived home safely, could be killed on our highways.

After a period of shock when the small community of Black Hills rallied around me with support, I began to make the changes necessary to continue on. I quit my job as a personnel trainer with the state of Washington and began the work it would take to open up my shop.

Once the shop was established, I began to look for ways to expand my horizons and fiber fairs were a very attractive option. So, for the last two years The Spider's Web has sponsored a booth here at the Gathering. I've sold products from my store and made contacts that helped me throughout the year. I've also found the time to peruse the fleeces that were on sale and usually picked up two or three for my own spinning. One of the big sellers at my shop has been my own handspun yarn.

Still wondering about the strange woman, I went to look for Rex to get the location of my booth and the stall for my alpaca. I soon found him in deep conversation with a volunteer who was wondering where she should set up the table to sell the Gathering's tee and sweatshirts. They decided on a location just inside the door and Rex, running his fingers through his gray hair and pushing it back off his forehead, turned toward me.

"Hi, Martha, hope you aren't the bearer of bad news too," he said.

"Nope, I just need to know where you've stuck me."

"You have good spots, I think. Your booth is right here," he said, pointing to a spot on a diagram of the arena. "The Great Pyrenees booth is right next to you, and they are next to one of the side doors."

"That's perfect, Rex. I really appreciate being next to the Pyr booth. Where do you have Juan and Joseph located?"

"They're over here." He pointed to another location on the diagram. "I have them located between some of the sheep and the llamas. I figure they are used to sheep and shouldn't have a problem with the larger camelids."

"They should be fine there," I said. "It looks like you have them in one of the permanent horse stalls. That should be plenty large."

"Actually, you have two of those stalls. I wasn't sure how much room they would need."

"Ah, Rex, I think we may have solved your stall problems if you want to be nice," I said.

Rex gave me a quizzical look. "I guess I'm not sure what you mean," he said.

"Let's go look at those stalls. If they're as large as I remember them, I will only need one, and you can give my extra one to that very angry woman who almost ran me down a little while ago."

"I'm not sure I want to give in to Catalin. But you're right; it would make my life much nicer this weekend if I could give her another stall. Let's go look at them."

The stalls were as large as I remembered them. One could easily hold my two alpaca and they would be happier together. Alpaca don't like being solitary. They really prefer company.

"You can have the second one back, Rex," I said. "The boys will prefer being together anyway. So let Catalin put her sheep in the one next to them."

"Thanks, Martha. You're a peach. I'll let her know that she has the additional stall because you gave it up."

"Hey, Rex." Janet, the fleece sale chairman was calling to him.

"Looks like I have another fire to put out," he said with a grin. "Thanks again, Martha."

"No problem. Go get your work done. I need to get this stall ready for my guys and get them moved in."

Rex walked over to where Janet was waiting and I headed

out to my pickup to get the straw I needed for bedding in the stall.

I soon had the alpaca settled in with plenty of food and water for the evening, and it was time to start the real work—setting up the booth for The Spider's Web.

Chapter 2

As I was working my way along the stalls in the main arena, I stopped to look at a really beautiful ewe. She had a glossy, lovely fleece and everything about her looked healthy and well cared for. Next to her were three lovely lambs in the same great condition. I checked the information on her, thinking that the rancher might be a source for another member of my flock if I decided to add to it. She came from Catalin Ranch; she belonged to Catalin. Just then I heard a cell phone and out of habit checked to see if it was mine. Nope, but I knew who it belonged to. That voice was becoming very noticeable today.

"Of course I'm not home. This is the weekend of the Black Hills Fiber Gathering. No, I'm not coming home until Sunday evening. No, I have no intention of meeting you in Olympia. Look, they haven't even been dead a month. You could have the decency to let some people grieve and to let them get settled

in their graves. I don't give a damn about the money and neither should you. Look, I'm not signing papers this weekend and
that's that. No, I don't want to hear it. No."

I heard her cell phone flip shut and she leaned over another
stall. She hadn't noticed me and I decided that this wasn't the
time to talk to her about her flock. I turned and went the other
way; there was more than one path to the parking lot. I heard
her cell phone ring again, but this time she didn't bother to
answer it.

I made my way quickly to my parking spot where I had the
front of the horse trailer loaded with tubs, tables, shelves, spinning wheels and one small loom for demonstrations. I loaded
up a dolly with the tables and shelves and headed back to the
booth space. It was an advantage that I was near a side door. I
didn't have to weave my way through all the other vendors setting up to get to my spot.

"I wondered where you were," a voice said as I walked
through the door. I looked up to see my best friend, Ellen, un-
loading at the Pyr booth. "I need your help getting this lattice
board set up," she continued.

"Will do, just let me put this stuff in my space."

The Pyr club had a booth every year at the Black Hills Fiber
Gathering. It was our best time to educate ranchers on the val-
ue of Great Pyrenees as livestock guardian dogs. We would also
talk to lots of the general public this weekend, but our focus was
the ranching community. Ellen was booth chair this year.

"OK, tell me what I need to do," I said as I walked over to
where Ellen was working.

"We need to set this lattice work up so I can hang pictures
from it. Once we have it vertical, I can use the bungees to attach
it to the hooks on the wall and stabilize it."

With a little work, we moved the large lattice trifold into position and opened up the wings. This helped stabilize it some. Then while I held it in position, Ellen reached up and hooked the bungees to the hooks that were in the wall of the arena building. Why they were there was a mystery, but they sure served our purpose well.

"There, that should hold it," Ellen said as she moved to the front of the lattice.

"Good thing you were here. I couldn't reach those without a ladder."

"Height does help," she said with a grin.

My best friend was almost six feet tall and willowy, and she moved with the grace of the dancer that she once was. While my Celtic heritage showed in my waist-length auburn hair, fair skin and freckles, Ellen's olive skin, single eye fold, and long black hair told nothing of her known English and Swedish heritage, but it made for my friend being one beautiful woman.

At this point, I heard a small protest bark and looked to the back of the booth where the crates for the Gathering were placed. Walking to the front of the crate, I saw the source of that bark. Shasta was standing there with her nose pressed against the crate door and her tail wagging. She was obviously ready to get out and meet and greet.

"And what are you doing here today, young lady?" I asked.

"She had to go to the vet for her rabies shot today. I didn't want to take the time to return her home," Ellen answered.

"Well, let's set up the exercise pen, then she can get out front where she can see the world. Obviously the shot hasn't affected her at all."

"That's probably the best solution," Ellen said. "I'll get it set up if you will take her out to go potty while I'm doing it."

"No problem. Come on big girl. Let's get you out of here."

I put a leash on Shasta, and we headed for the great outdoors. Immediately, her nose went on the ground as she investigated all the new smells. I walked her behind one of the stable buildings where there was a small patch of grass.

"Come on, girl, it's time to go potty."

Just as she squatted, her head came up and her attention was diverted to voices around the corner of the building.

"I swear I'm going to kill that woman yet. Not only is she making my life miserable with trying to steal my property, but now she's causing trouble here."

"Now, it can't be that bad. Does she have any grounds for the land dispute?"

"Not as far as I know, but she's still taking up my time and resources while we fight our way through this thing."

"It will work out. Just relax and don't let her get to you this weekend. You have enough on your plate with the Gathering as it is."

"I guess so. She started in on me first thing this afternoon, but Martha Williamson saved me by giving up a stall."

That told me who one of the speakers was. I wondered who Rex was talking to and just how serious his dispute with Catalin was. Well, I obviously wasn't meant to be party to this conversation, and Shasta had completed her business, so it was time I turned around and returned to the arena. Besides, I hadn't even started setting up my booth.

"Come on, Shasta, it's time to put you away and for me to get to work."

"I was about to send out a search party for the two of you," Ellen said as we walked in.

As I put Shasta in the exercise pen, I filled Ellen in on the conversation that I'd just heard and Rex's earlier one with Catalin.

"Sounds like Rex has his hands full everywhere right now," Ellen commented. "At least we can do our part to make his life easier."

"Yep, and the best way to do that at the moment is to get these booths set up and ready to go. It looks like you're about ready, but I have a long way to go."

"I just need to get a couple of pictures hung and I'll be in a position to help you. I won't put the handouts and books out until tomorrow."

I started arranging tables and shelves and soon had them where I wanted them. Now I just had a dozen plastic tubs to empty out to fill those shelves. But I'd have to get them first.

"OK, what can I do?" Ellen asked.

"As soon as I get back from the truck with my inventory, you can help me fill these shelves. Want to walk out with me?"

"Do you need my help out there?"

"Nope."

"Then, I'll stay in here and keep an eye on this girl."

"OK, be back in a jiff."

I went back out the side door to avoid the stops that walking along the vendors would cause and soon had most of the stuff loaded up and was hauling it back in.

"Here," I said when I saw Ellen, "you can start putting these books, magazines and patterns on the shelves over here, and I'll go back out for the last haul."

"Will do."

It didn't take long to retrieve my final load of supplies, including the larger items, and I was back in the booth to help Ellen.

"Take this tub and place the skeins of handspun and the roving on that table. I'll start placing the knitting needles, spindles, and other small tools on the shelves over here. Then we can put the commercial skeins on the shelves near the handspun. I'll use the other table for the loom, carder and other large items."

We made progress rapidly and soon the booth looked like it might be ready for business the next morning.

"Well, aren't you a pretty one."

The voice was familiar but the whole tone was different. I turned to see Catalin crouched down, talking to Shasta. Shasta seemed enamored with her and was trying to give her snuffles through the exercise pen.

"Her name is Shasta," I commented.

"She's lovely. Is she yours?"

"No, she belongs to me." Ellen appeared from behind the table where she had been filling lower shelves.

"Is she usually a working dog?"

"Yes, she's here because of a veterinary appointment. She's learning to work with my male guarding a small flock."

"Well, they do their job well. I have eight of them working in pairs in my pastures. Since they arrived, I've had no wild predator kills. I did have a dog pack attack that managed to do damage two years ago when they injured my male and basically overpowered the female that was with him."

"Dogs are by far the biggest problem where I live. I'm just outside of town and other than coyotes, we seldom see wild predators. But dogs often do damage to flocks that aren't protected," I chimed in.

"Mine is a mix," Catalin said, "but the dogs are the most dangerous. The mountain lions and bears will usually give a flock with dogs a wide berth. Coyotes are always opportunists but they too don't like the dogs. It is only the pets that couldn't possibly hurt anything that cause the real damage."

"Yes," Ellen added, "and it is so hard to convince people that their dog is much better off with a fence and boundaries. Just because they now live in the country doesn't mean that their dog should be allowed to run free."

"And we're all three preaching to the choir," I said.

"Amen, sister," Catalin added. "By the way, thanks for giving up one of your stalls. I really appreciate it. Rex really managed to screw things up and I was fit to be tied."

"Glad I could be of help."

Catalin crouched down to Shasta. "Well, pretty girl, you do a good job for your mom, you hear." Then she turned to us as she got up. "I'm sure I'll see you around this weekend. Good luck with your sales."

"Thanks," I said. "I hope you manage to sell your lambs."

"Me too," she said as she turned to walk further down the line of booths.

"Well, that was sure a different person," I said to Ellen.

"She sure was. She's obviously better with animals and with people when she can have animals front for her. And Shasta thought she was pretty special. Where do you want me to put this silk?" Ellen continued, bringing us back to the task at hand.

"Oh, that is handspun and should go over here. Better yet, let's put it by the silk roving so that people can see what their roving might look like if they buy it."

"OK. Things look good to me, Martha; I think your offerings get better each year."

"Thanks. Yep, I think we're done here. I'll leave the wheels and looms under the tables until tomorrow morning. I'll just cover things with sheets for protection then we can take Shasta to check on Juan and Joseph and get out of here. Want to come over for dinner?"

"It sounds good but I have programming to do if I'm going to be here all day tomorrow, and Shasta's had a big day too. I think I'll take a rain check. But we'll walk over to see the alpaca with you. That would be good for her. She hasn't been up close and personal with anything that big."

Ellen is a freelance computer programmer and a good one, so I could understand that she might have work to do.

"Sounds good to me. Help me spread the sheets, and I'm ready to go."

It took us quite awhile to get to the stall with Juan and Joseph in it because Shasta had to stop and say hi to each person and animal we met along the way. She was obviously in her element and delighted with life and her adventures for the day. Ellen and I were busy talking to each other when Shasta stopped short. Her head cocked, her ears elevated and her nose went up. She'd just spotted the alpaca.

"Hey, you silly goose, what do you think?" Ellen asked as I opened the stall so Shasta could get a better look.

She looked up at Ellen and then back at the alpaca. Then, head lowered properly for approaching livestock, she moved toward the big critters. When she got within kicking distance, she stopped. Smart little girl. She looked at them again and gave a gentle woof. Juan and Joseph, who were used to Great Pyrenees, lowered their heads to sniff her. At that point I wished I'd had my camera because they were soon nose to nose and Shasta's tail was moving slowly back and forth. She then let out a little snort and moved back to take another look at them. Juan and Joseph, who figured they'd been introduced, moved over to where I had just placed some grain for them. Food was obviously more interesting than this small white creature. Shasta looked back up at Ellen and then tugged on her leash as if to say, let's move on and see what else is out here.

"So much for the attention span of a puppy," Ellen said with a laugh.

"Well, these two look settled for the night. Let's follow her example and take ourselves home too."

Talking as always, Ellen and I worked our way toward the door. Just as we got there, we once again heard angry voices and one sounded familiar. I looked at Ellen and we moved around a pillar to see what was going on.

"How dare you sell my lambs!" An angry young black woman with a short cap of dark, tight curls around her head confronted Catalin. "Those lambs are mine. Just because you won't let me come get them doesn't negate that fact." Her voice was low and melodious, but you could feel her anger in the timbre of it.

"Your lambs, your lambs, your lambs." Catalin's voice rose with each repeat of the phrase. "They were born on my ranch; they are my lambs."

"They were born on our ranch, and these came from my ewe."

"It was only our ranch when you had a part in my life. You've lost that with your unfaithfulness. No longer is it a part of you."

Catalin seemed to tower over the other woman who was a good three to four inches shorter. Her anger radiated out of her and her face was contorted.

"I'm not going over this with you again here in public," the young black woman said, "but I never did anything but try to point out the injustices that you were causing."

"You took his side against me," Catalin snapped back. "You betrayed my trust and our love."

"Never except to you."

"Bullshit. You lie."

"I've never lied to you, Catalin. That's probably the problem right now. But I want you to know that I'll get what is mine from our life together and you can't keep it from me."

"I can, and I will."

"Just know that whatever it takes, I will prevail." With that last comment, the stranger turned on her heel and walked away from Catalin.

Catalin stood looking after her, her face a picture of anger, but there was something else there too. Could it have been pain?

Ellen and I just shook our heads and walked out of the arena before we commented.

"That woman seems to carry anger with her," Ellen said after a minute.

"She does. Yet, she was so gentle with Shasta, and I watched her with her sheep when I was taking care of the alpaca and she was the perfect shepherd. It's almost as if she were two different people."

"It is. However, remind me to give her a wide berth," Ellen added. "I don't want to be in the crosshairs of that anger."

"Me either. Well, here's my truck. If you're sure you don't want to stop for dinner, I'll see you in the morning."

"It's time for me to get this young one home and get started on my real work. I'll be here early to open up, so I'll see you then."

I gave Ellen a hug and watched as she continued down the parking lot to her truck. Then I got into mine and headed home. It had been a long afternoon and because of the anger that Catalin seemed to spew everywhere a more stressful one than usual.

I didn't know either Catalin or the black woman, but I surmised that they had a longstanding relationship, probably a lesbian one from the sounds of it. From the pain that I thought I glimpsed on Catalin's face and the tone in the other woman's voice, I bet they both wanted that life back. They just didn't know how to bridge the anger. I hoped they would find a way.

Chapter 3

I had to drive through Black Hills on my way home. Our small town is mainly a wide place in the road that once served timber families as home. With the downturn of the timber industry, it had become a bedroom community for Olympia, the state capital, and a place where tourists stop for a quick bite to eat, obtain gas or find lodging. My farm's at the west end of Black Hills Road which makes a loop off State Highway 8 to get into the town.

It didn't take me long to arrive home, and I was greeted by barking Pyrs as I pulled into my driveway. Denali and Falcor, my two Great Pyrenees, were letting me know that I'd been noticed. Good dogs.

I climbed out of my truck and looked around. I still marveled in the beauty of this land that I was able to call mine. John and I had chosen well when we settled here. After his death, I made changes. I had a new barn built for my animals and turned the wonderful old barn into The Spider's Web. About half of the acreage was securely fenced for pasture for my small spinners flock. The rest was a forest of Douglas fir, vine maple, and pine. A small stream ran through the back of the property and it was a favorite walk for the dogs and me when we had a quiet moment to enjoy it.

I wasn't expecting anyone for the evening so I decided to close my gate for the night. One thing that every Pyr owner knows is you never let them see open territory. They will leave to check all the territory they can see, much of which may not be yours. So I had my property fenced to keep the Pyrs securely back with the animals during the day. Then with the outer gate closed, I could give them free range of the complete property and the house in the evening.

With the front gate closed, I walked over to where the Pyrs were waiting for me. They gave me a quick sniff-over, accepted a pat as their due, then went out to mark and investigate the territory that they had been excluded from all day. Having fulfilled their duties in the front, they joined me as I made my way to the barn to take care of my animals for the night.

I have a small spinning flock. I should have probably sold at least the boy from this year's lambs at the Gathering, but I couldn't bring myself to part with him, so he was castrated and will stay with me. He's pure Jacob and has lovely colors. His fleece will be a good addition to my supply. My other sheep include his mother, Lehua, a Jacob ewe, and her second lamb, Lei, Koa, an Icelandic wether, Lani and her two lambs, Ginger and Maile, who were Corriedale crosses, and Hoku and Pua, Shetland ewes.

All the Hawaiian names were reminders of the years that John and I lived in Hawai`i. The military had brought me full circle with that duty station, as my father was stationed at Hickam AFB in Honolulu when I was born. The last member of the flock was Coco an angora goat who needed a companion. Maybe I'll look for one at the Gathering.

Soon, I had everyone fed and bedded down. It seemed odd to not have the Alpaca there, but I knew they were safe in the stall at the Gathering.

"I'm leaving; you going with me?" I said to the Pyrs. They just looked up from their own dinner and wagged their tails to say they'd be in later after they'd finished. So with one last check of the barn, I turned out the lights, closed the doors, and headed for the house and my own dinner. The Pyrs had their own door, which gave them the ability to come and go as they pleased.

I climbed the steps to the back porch and was met by Samantha, who let me know as only a Siamese cat can that she was displeased with me.

"Hey, pretty lady, are you hungry?"

"Yowaah!"

"You are. OK, let's go in and feed you."

I shed my shoes and walked in the door. That was another part of Hawai`i that had stuck. I seldom ever wore shoes into the house even in this colder climate. Samantha intertwined my legs while serenading me with her complaints about my slowness.

"OK, OK, here it is," I said as I placed her food on the counter in the laundry room. This wasn't foolproof for keeping Pyr noses out of it, but it worked most of the time.

Although we were in mid-May, it was a bit chilly tonight so I decided to build a fire before I started my dinner. I have a large country kitchen and love the fact that there is a two-sided fireplace that separates the kitchen and dining area from the living room. I can enjoy a cheery fire during the long evenings of a Northwest winter no matter which room I'm in. I soon had a fire going and went to check the fridge for something to eat. I had some leftover roasted chicken from yesterday that I could nuke, and there was a leftover baked potato that could be turned into home fries. With some tomato and cucumber slices for veggies, I'd have a reasonably balanced dinner. Soon, I was settled on a cushion in front of the fireplace using my large redwood coffee table as a dining table. With some Hawaiian music playing in the background, I let my mind wander back to those lovely walks on the beach with John. It had been four years, but I still missed him.

However, recently I had begun to entertain thoughts of a new relationship for the first time. Following Denali's close shave with death when a murderer took a wild shot at her and Falcor, I had started seeing my veterinarian for more than professional reasons. Mark would probably be at the Gathering tomorrow since he would be the vet on call. It would be good to see him because our busy lives had made it impossible to get together for the past week.

Having finished my dinner, I reached for the Cat Who book that I was reading and curled up there on the floor with Samantha on my lap. Unlike Ko Ko and Yum Yum, she had no desire for me to read aloud, but she did like to lap sit. Lost in the world of Jim Qwilleran and his feline companions, I came to with a start when Samantha jumped up as a Pyr nose reached over to snuffle her. She only tolerated the big white dogs and now stomped off leaving my lap for the solitude of the window seat.

"Hi, big girl, you want some attention too. Huh?"

A slow wave of a tail and a paw were my answers. I reached up and scratched Denali's ears and she settled down beside me. She wouldn't stay long as the fire would get too warm, but for now she was glad to be beside me. I returned to my book until Nali got up and padded off for the spot next to the back door, and I noticed that the fire had burned down. It was time for me to head for bed.

I gathered up my dishes and took them to the dishwasher. With a quick cleanup and setting up of the coffee, the kitchen was ready for morning.

I gave Denali a goodnight pat and headed into the bedroom. I'd leave the bedroom door open in case the dogs wanted to come in during the night. As in the barn and the shop, there was a dog door into my laundry room to give the dogs access to the house. They'd move between the house, the barn and the property throughout the night making sure that all was safe from predators both four and two footed. I'd sleep well under their watchful care.

Chapter 4

A cold nose nuzzled my ear and I rolled over to look at the clock. It was just a little after five o'clock.

"You think it's time for me to get up, Falcor?"

Another nuzzle was my answer.

"OK, OK, I'm coming. Do you know that you're going with me today and that's why you are so sure that I should get up early?"

For this question, I just got a look as he turned and went out the door. He'd be waiting outside to escort me to the barn. I pulled on my sweats and socks. They would do for barn duty. I turned on the coffee as I walked through the kitchen and, grabbing my coat, I walked out onto the back porch. The sky was starting to turn a pale rose and it looked like we might have a beautiful day for the opening of the Gathering. That would be nice. People and animals slogging through mud did not make for a wonderful experience.

"OK, let's go take care of your charges. Where's Nali?"

On cue, she trotted out from behind the barn and came over to join Falcor and me as we entered the door.

"You've got guard duty by yourself today, Nali. Think you're up to it?"

She answered with a slow wag of her tail and what I could have sworn was a smile. It was only recently that I'd let her take on full-time guard duty again. Following the gunshot wound in February, I'd wanted to make sure she was totally recovered before I put her out to handle any predators that might come along. But day watch was usually easier and she'd been declared totally fit by Mark, so I figured I could take Falcor with me today. Tomorrow, she'd be allowed to go with me and he'd stay home to guard.

Lani looked up and bleated as I approached the feeding area and pulled down hay for the sheep and Coco, the goat. Once they had feed, I opened the large doors to the pasture. They would wander out after they'd eaten and spend most of their day out there. I checked the watering trough outside the doors and topped it off. With that done, I fed the hens, gathered the eggs, and called Falcor to come with me. Nali followed us to the inner gate but knew she was to stay inside this morning. I closed the gate behind Falcor and me. He looked back at Nali, and then turned around and followed me out to pick up the paper.

The coffee smelled wonderful as I walked into the kitchen but Samantha let it be known that she must be fed before I poured myself a cup. Having fed her, I could think about breakfast for me. Because food at the Gathering would be catch as catch can, I figured that I should probably eat pretty well this morning. I turned on KPLU to catch Morning Edition, poured myself that cup of coffee, and scrambled some eggs with ham. The addition of a couple of pieces of toast and some orange slices completed my fare for the morning. I gathered up my plate to carry it to the table and picked up The Olympian to read while I ate my breakfast. I'm not a news junkie but I do like to have at least a vague idea of what's going on. I noticed that Rex had managed to get a small article on the Gathering into the paper. Good, that should bring in more customers.

A glance at the clock told me that I needed to hustle if I was going to get to the Gathering in plenty of time to take care of Juan and Joseph before people started arriving. I'd soon finished my shower and pulled on a pair of jeans, a light hand-knit sweater and some hand-knit socks. I pulled my hair into a single braid down my back and applied the small amount of makeup I wear. Gathering up my purse, keys and jacket and slipping my feet into low-heeled boots, I called to Falcor and headed for my van.

It took no prompting to get Falcor to jump into his crate once I had the van and crate door open. He loved going on rides and didn't really care where the final destination was.

"OK, big guy, we're off and running," I said as I climbed back into the van after closing the outside gate behind us. My only answer was the sound of Falcor turning around and laying down in the crate for the ride.

I was early enough that I was able to get a parking place fairly close to the arena building. That would make it easy in case I wanted to give Falcor a rest from the crowd and let him sleep in the van for awhile. Of course, I could also put him in the stall with Juan and Joseph; and I might do that for part of the day.

The arena was quiet when I entered except for the occasional bleat of a sheep. But as Falcor and I moved toward where Juan and Joseph were staying, I heard the humming of a llama and it didn't sound happy. As I came even with the alpaca's stall, Falcor pulled on the leash.

"What is it, big guy?"

He answered with another pull. As this wasn't standard behavior for him, I decided to let him have his way, and I followed him further down the walkway in front of the stalls. He brought me to the llama's stall and stood outside of it.

"What, Falcor? Can you tell what's bothering the llama? Let's see if we can do any..."

That last word stuck in my throat as I looked into the llama's stall. There on the floor lay a body, and unless there was more than one person at the Gathering with a long black braid wrapped around her head, it was Catalin.

"Falcor, down."

I looped his leash over a post and opened the door to the stall. The llama was in the back humming loudly.

"It's OK, big guy; we'll get you out of here in just a minute. You stay back there while I check on your unwanted company. You're a good boy," I continued to talk to the llama in an effort to calm him as I knelt beside Catalin. There was no pulse, and her body was cool. She'd been here awhile.

I pulled my cell phone out of my pocket and dialed 911.

"Emergency operator. How may I help you?"

"This is Martha Williamson. There's been a terrible accident at the Black Hills Riding Academy Arena. We need Jonathon and an ambulance."

"I'm dispatching them now. Will you please stay on the line until they arrive?"

"Yes, I will."

Just then another animal owner came to the front of the stall. Falcor stood and blocked her access to the stall, but he couldn't block the vision of Catalin on the floor.

"Oh, my God! What's wrong! Why aren't you helping her? Make that dog let me in there."

"No, you can't help in here," I said, "but you can help by going to find Rex and getting him over here pronto. And don't tell anyone else. We don't need a crowd here any sooner than it's going to happen anyway."

"But she's hurt. Why aren't you doing anything?"

"She's not hurt. She's dead. Please go get Rex."

"How do you know? Are you a doctor? Surely you can do something."

"I've done something. I've called an ambulance and the authorities. Go get Rex; that is the best help you can be."

"But...."

"Go get Rex. Now."

"OK, but," she continued as she gave me a dirty look and turned on her heel to find Rex.

"Good boy, Falcor. You continue to guard."

Just then the llama started to shift and I had to turn my attention to him once more. I had no desire to be caught by surprise and injured myself by a sudden move on his part.

"Gentle there, big guy, we'll get you out of here as soon as I can get a halter and lead for you."

"What are you doing in my llama's stall?" came an angry voice from a short distance down the row of stalls.

"There's been..."

"Good God, lady, what's going on here?" A tall, muscular man with long red hair pulled back in a ponytail and snappy green eyes was confronting me from the other side of Falcor, who had stood up again and raised his hackles. He obviously didn't like the man's tone.

"I don't know. Your llama was humming in a manner that appeared to be distress. Falcor and I came down here and found this. Would you get a halter so you can remove him? He's obviously unhappy here."

He reached into his back pocket and pulled one out.

"I was ready to take him out for some exercise. Uh, could you tell your dog that I can join you?"

Falcor was still standing his ground and guarding both me and the stall.

"Falcor, let the man in. Good boy." Falcor moved aside but remained wary.

"Good animal you got there," he said as he walked in and over to his llama. "Come on, Pedro, it's OK."

The man gentled his friend, running his large hands over him and then slipped the halter on. The llama obviously relaxed with the gentle touch and voice of his owner. When he had his animal under control, he looked at the floor of the stall again.

"What in the hell happened here? How did Catalin get there?"

"Catalin, where are you? Why haven't you taken care of my lambs?"

A voice I recognized from the day before came from the stall next to Juan and Joseph.

"That's Sheila. If she sees Catalin, she's going to freak," the llama owner said.

"James, have you seen Catalin? She hasn't taken care of the lambs. That's not like her."

"Here, take this." The gentleman handed me the lead to the llama and walked out of the stall. Obviously he was James.

"Sheila, there's been an accident." His tone of voice was about the same as when he gentled his llama.

"What kind of accident? Where's Catalin?"

Sheila pushed past James and came to the front of the stall.

"Noooooooooo. What's happened to Catalin? Why aren't you helping her? Let me in! Let me get to her! Get that dog out of here!"

Falcor had once again taken up his post and was blocking Sheila's way.

"What the hell is going on here?" That voice was Rex. "Martha, that hysterical woman said something about a body. Oh shit." He had gotten close enough to see the llama and Catalin's body on the floor of the stall.

"Rex, make them let me in there. I need to go to Catalin. That woman isn't doing anything but holding that damn llama. I need to help Catalin."

"Sheila, come over here with me," James said as he put his arm around her. "We can't help Catalin and you need to sit down."

"What do you mean, we can't help her. Surely we can do something. James, let go of me and let me in there."

"Are you still there?"

I realized that I had forgotten the emergency dispatch operator who was still on my cell phone.

"Yes, I am. I assume you heard some of what's going on here."

"Yes, I did. I've relayed some of it to Jonathon who is pulling into the parking lot right now. He should be there in just a minute."

"OK, I'm going to hang up. He'll get everything under control. Thanks for your help."

"That's what we're here for."

I hung up and put my cell phone in my pocket just as

Jonathon started down the row of stalls. He moved quickly down the hallway with the balanced power of the aikido master that he was. Today his crooked grin was missing and he was obviously all business.

"Martha," he started to address me.

"That woman won't let me in to help Catalin. You've got to make her let me in."

Sheila pushed herself in front of Jonathon, who looked over her head to see into the stall. I quietly shook my head back and forth as he glanced at me and then took in the rest of the scene.

"I don't think you can help her, ma'am," he said gently. He looked up as James came up behind Sheila.

"Come on, Sheila. You can't help Catalin and Chief Green needs to get in there. But your lambs do need you. Remember Catalin didn't take care of them this morning. So maybe you and I can go take care of them. Will you continue to hold Pedro for a few minutes?" he continued to me.

"Yes, I can and I imagine that Jonathon wants him here for a few more minutes."

"I do want him to stay; and, Martha, will you tell Falcor that he can let me into the stall?"

"OK, Falcor, let Jonathon in."

Falcor moved aside and pushed Jonathon's hand for a pet. Jonathon was one of his favorite people but he knew he had a job to do this morning and that came first.

"Friends again, big guy," Jonathon said as he gave Falcor's ears a scratch. Falcor answered by slowly moving his tail and then once again positioned himself to block entrance into the stall.

Jonathon came over to examine the llama. Born and raised in Black Hills, Jonathon had been chief of police for over ten years. He had a solid reputation among the law enforcement community for his knowledge and skill, but it was his fairness and desire for justice that the people of Black Hills cherished.

"Let's look at you, Pedro, so we can get you out of this stall."

He gently ran his hands over the llama's neck and back then down along his withers. Pedro was quite a large male and powerfully built, and he wasn't terribly happy with Jonathon touching him. His ears went back and his head went up. However, even with this invasion of his space by a stranger, he still didn't seem ready to make an aggressive move. Was there any way that he could have contributed to Catalin's injuries?

Jonathon moved over to look at Catalin. He rolled her over and you could see where she had been wounded on the back of her head. It was a very large gash and the skull was broken. James had a tack box in the corner of the stall. It was fairly large and metal. There was blood on the corner of the box. Was that the cause of Catalin's head wound? Could the llama have caught her off balance in some way and knocked her over so that she hit her head? Was that what had happened?

"Where's Jonathon?" I heard a voice from down by the door.

"Down here," Jonathon said as he stood up so he could be seen.

"I suppose you've had a ton of people in here stomping around," the woman said as she came into view of the stall where Falcor stopped her from entering.

"Nope," said Jonathon, "and you're looking at the reason why we haven't."

"Well, do you suppose you could tell him to let me in?"

"Martha," Jonathon said to me.

"OK, Falcor. You can let this one in." Falcor stood aside and then once more took his station after letting the woman in.

She was in her mid-forties, I would guess, and built solid and square. Her face was all angles and right now her frown took in her forehead, her eyes and her mouth. She obviously wasn't happy to see me in there with Jonathon either.

"And who are you?" She addressed this to me.

"Margaret, this is Martha Williamson. Martha, this is Margaret Yeager, the deputy coroner. Margaret, Martha found the body. The only person that Falcor has let into the stall besides the three of us was the llama's owner. He needed to get a halter and lead on his animal and get him calmed down initially."

"And where is he now?"

"He's down the row of stalls a bit, helping to calm down the partner of the dead woman. He has her taking care of her lambs in an effort to keep her distracted and out of our hair."

"Hmph. Well, let me see what we have here. Have you moved anything?"

"I rolled Catalin over," Jonathon said. "Other than that and the moving around that the llama has done, nothing has been disturbed."

"The llama was up against the back of the stall and in obvious distress when I arrived this morning," I added. "As a matter of fact, it was his noise and distress that caused Falcor to want to come down here and see what was happening. Otherwise, I would have stopped a couple of stalls up the row where my alpaca are housed."

Margaret knelt down and examined Catalin.

"It looks like she died from the blow to her head, but we'll need an autopsy to know for sure."

"I'm thinking that the llama must have shoved Catalin in some manner and caught her off balance. Maybe she spooked him enough to have him bump her rather hard and cause her to fall, hitting her head on that tack box," Jonathon said. "It seems that Catalin was the victim of a terrible accident."

Margaret glanced over at Catalin again, and then examined the stall. She seemed satisfied to look at Pedro only from a distance. Obviously the large animal made her nervous.

"Look at this," Margaret said. She had knelt to look at Catalin more closely and directed Jonathon's gaze toward Catalin's large ring.

"It looks like hair of some sort, maybe from the llama," she continued.

"It doesn't look quite right for llama fiber," I chimed in.

"And I suppose you're the expert." She turned to me. I think she'd half forgotten that I was standing there still holding Pedro.

"Well, actually she is," Jonathon responded. "She owns a spinning and weaving shop, and her job is fiber."

"I'll take this ring and we can let the forensic people decide what it is," Margaret said without really giving on her opinion.

"Can I take my llama now?" James said as he walked up.

"I'm sorry," Jonathon said, "but we're pretty sure that he accidentally killed Catalin in some kind of an attack. I'm going to have to put him into quarantine."

"Quarantine. Does that mean you're going to take him and just stuff him away in some hole of a stable? This is a valuable animal. He's also extremely gentle. I use him for children's rides at the fair. He wouldn't hurt a fly, let alone Catalin Ezkarra. This woman was second generation Basque. She managed to get on the wrong side of most people on a regular basis but she could do anything with an animal. They calmed down when she walked near them. There is no way that Catalin could have been killed by an animal. Nope, I don't know what happened, but Pedro didn't kill her."

"You've really got to be kidding," Sheila chimed in. She had walked up with James. "Catalin could calm a fighting stallion," Sheila continued. "There's no way a llama in a stall would have wanted to kill her, let alone been able to. I don't know what happened, but I can tell you that it wasn't Pedro."

"Well, all the evidence points that way," said Jonathon, "so the llama goes into quarantine. It isn't just any stable though. He will go over to Mark Begay's stable at his clinic."

Mark was the only large animal veterinarian in the area and he had a small stable for animals that he was treating.

"Well, I don't like it, but at least I know Mark'll take good care of him. However, Jonathon, I suggest that you keep looking. Whatever this was, it wasn't an accident caused by my llama."

"Can we get through, please?" said a young medic.

I looked up to see that we had gathered quite a large crowd as more and more shepherds and vendors had arrived for the day. I looked at my watch and realized that we would also have the general public arriving soon for the Gathering.

"Margaret, are you ready for us to take the body?"

"It's not a body. It's Catalin. At least give her the respect of a name," Sheila said. Her voice had lost its edge of hysteria and had picked up some of the melody again but it was still rough around the edges with stress. "Can I go with her?" she asked.

"No, she's going to the morgue for an autopsy. The body will be released to the next of kin when it's done. I'm assuming that isn't you," Margaret said as she eyed Sheila and her skin color.

Sheila just looked at her and shook her head as her eyes filled with tears. Rex stepped forward and gathered the distraught woman into his arms.

"Come on, Sheila, you can't do anything more here. Do you

want someone to drive you home?"

"Home? Where's home? I had hoped that Catalin and I could get things sorted out. Oh Rex, what am I going to do?"

"You'll do what you have to. You're a strong woman, and in spite of the last few weeks, Catalin loved you. She would want you to carry on and take care of the animals that are here. I'll see if I can get one of my men over to make sure the ones on the ranch are OK."

"You're right. No one will allow me to grieve anyway. After all, our relationship wasn't supposed to be. I guess I should just go back to work as if my heart wasn't torn out right now."

"Now, Sheila, that bitterness isn't you."

This last came from James. Sheila just looked at him, turned on her heel and walked with her head down toward the stall with her lambs in it.

"She's torn apart," Rex said to me as I continued to watch her walk away. "They've been together for twenty years. I think they'd have patched things up. They each loved the other very much. Sheila could see past Catalin's anger to the gentle woman that she was inside. Catalin relied on Sheila to be her public side with people. They balanced each other quite well, as many couples do."

"It's too bad that the law doesn't acknowledge that relationship. Does Catalin have next of kin?"

"A brother and a nephew. She and the brother are estranged, I think. She sees quite a bit of the nephew. I suppose I should see if I can find the brother's name for Jonathon. I think I might have it in my computer someplace."

"May I take Pedro for a walk?" James surprised me and I realized that I was still holding the llama's lead.

"I suppose so," Jonathon replied. "Just don't take him far.

I've called Mark and he's on his way with a trailer to pick him up."

"Where do I put him when I bring him back in," James said. "I know from what Rex said yesterday, there are no spare stalls."

"There are three of Sheila's lambs in the stall next to Juan and Joseph. It's a large stall, I bet he could stay there for a short time. That is, if he's good with sheep," I added.

"He's fine with sheep. That's a good idea. I'll put him in there. Sheila won't mind, I know."

"Speaking of Juan and Joseph, I haven't cared for them at all. Do you need me for anything more, Jonathon?"

"No, the body's going now. I think you've helped as much as you can, Martha."

"What about the Gathering?" Rex asked. "What do I do about it?"

"Well, this was a tragic accident but I think you can go on with the Gathering. I'm going to tape off this stall, though, and I don't want anyone in it for now. I want to make sure we have all the information we need before you clean it up."

"Thanks. I'll get a sign to put up, and if you put some police tape on it, people should stay out."

"Then I really do need to take care of my animals, and I still have some setting up to do at my booth."

"OK, people," Jonathon said to those of the crowd that still remained around the stall. The show's over. All of you have work to do. Go do it, and let the medics pass."

The people slowly made way for the gurney with the body bag on it and then moved on to where they also had animals and booths to take care of.

"Come on, Falcor," I said to the dog who had been patiently

lying down once he felt that his need for guarding was over. "You've been a big help this morning. Now we need to go take care of Juan and Joseph."

I walked down to my stall and Juan and Joseph started humming before I got there. Falcor moved ahead of me and waited for me to open the door to the stall. Then he slipped in and put his nose up against Juan's. He seemed to be saying, "It's all right now."

I went over each of the alpaca quickly with my hands just to make sure that all was well with them. Alpaca aren't groomed in the sense that a horse or dog would be. Brushing can damage the fiber. I checked their food and added some more hay. I filled their water buckets and cleaned up the area in the corner of their stall where they had pooped. Alpaca are very clean animals and they had confined this to just one area of the stall. That made cleanup easier. With that done, my boys were ready to face the crowd for the day. I made sure that the "Do Not Pet" sign was clearly visible on the door of the stall.

"Do you want to stay in here for awhile, big guy?" Falcor answered me by laying down right inside the stall door. No person was going to give his alpaca any trouble while he was there. "OK, I'll be back later to get you."

With my animals taken care of, I turned and headed for my booth.

Chapter 5

I didn't expect you to be as late as I am," Ellen said as I walked up to the booth and saw her just starting to unpack. "And what's going on? I saw police vehicles in the parking lot."

I filled her in on the events of the morning.

"That will teach me to oversleep. I come in late and miss all the excitement."

"I'd just as soon have missed it too," I said. "Falcor, by the way, was a champ. He kept all comers out of the stall until I said it was OK. It was a big help in keeping the scene in good shape for Jonathon and the deputy coroner. However, I think they've missed the boat on their verdict. That llama was very gentle, and from what I understand and based on what we saw yesterday with Shasta, Catalin was a whiz with animals. Not good with people but great with animals. So why would a gentle llama attack her? Nope, I think something else happened."

"From what you've said, it sounds that way to me too. And

it sounded like both James and Sheila felt the same way." Ellen continued, "Now James has a vested interest in feeling that way, but Sheila doesn't."

"But if the llama didn't kill her, who did? We know she and Rex were having differences and so were she and Sheila. But I can't imagine Rex killing anyone, and Sheila was devastated today when she found out that Catalin was dead. Or at least she appeared to be."

"That's a good question. Catalin seemed to have annoying people down to an art. I wonder if she managed to anger some-one else enough to cause them to kill her."

"I don't know," I said, but I do know that I need to get my booth ready to go. People are starting to wander in with buying on their minds."

I pulled the spinning wheels out from under the tables. I had three with me. Two were samples for people to try. The third was mine. I'd use it during slow periods. It could be both a demon-stration and allow me to get some yarn done at the same time. I also pulled out the small Ashford Knitter's Loom. This is a cute little rigid heddle loom that folds up for easy carrying. I had it set up with a warp so that customers could try weaving on it.

I'd just finished setting up and was sitting down to my wheel when I saw Jonathon coming down the aisle toward my booth.

"Hey, Ellen, where's that pup of yours?" he said, passing me and stopping at the Pyr booth.

"Home guarding her sheep with Tahoma. You'll have to settle for this big girl," Ellen said as she came forward with a lovely Pyr bitch that belonged to one of the club members.

"And what is your name, pretty lady?" Jonathon said as he crouched down to pet the dog who had sat and raised her paw to get his attention.

"She's Pele. Her owner's around here somewhere, but I'd gladly take her if the owner doesn't come back."

"Enough of that kind of talk, Ellen. We've had one too many accidents already this morning."

"You know, Jonathon," I chimed in, "I have real problems with the llama killing Catalin. He's gentle and she was known for her animal expertise."

"Now, Martha, don't go turning cop on me again. Last time we came damn close to losing you and Denali. Police work is for the professionals. Although, I'll give Falcor a lot of credit for his crowd control this morning. It was a big help."

"I'm not trying to get in your way, Jonathon; but that llama killing her just doesn't make sense."

"Well, it appears that way now and that's the way I'm going to go unless we get evidence from the autopsy that indicates otherwise. In the meantime, I need to locate her brother and let him know about her death."

"Is that her next of kin—a brother?"

"Yes, according to Rex and Sheila, her parents were killed in a car accident recently. She had one brother and a nephew."

"I suppose that Sheila has no standing as next of kin," I commented.

"That's correct. At present, the law doesn't recognize their relationship. The brother could, of course, defer to her on decisions, but that would be up to him."

"So where's my sister?" A loud voice broke into our conversation.

All heads along the vending booths, including Jonathon's, Ellen's and mine turned to look toward the voice. A swarthy-skinned man who was just slightly taller than she glowered at Sheila. He repeated his question. "Where's my sister?"

Sheila seemed shocked. She was shaking her head and stepping back as if to get away from this rude person. Both Jonathon and I headed in that direction.

"May I help you?" Jonathon said as we came up to Sheila's booth.

"I'm looking for my sister, Catalin Ezkarra, and this bitch doesn't seem to be capable of telling me where she is. You'd think that after all these years, she could at least answer a question when I ask her."

"You are Mr. Ezkarra?" I asked.

"Didn't I just say that? If Catalin is my sister, I must be Mr. Ezkarra. Mr. Joseba Ezkarra, to be exact, and I don't have time to waste standing around here talking. I need to get her to sign these papers and get out of here."

"Mr. Ezkarra, I'm Jonathon Green. I'm the chief of police here in Black Hills. Would you mind walking over to the office with me? I need to talk to you."

"Well, then talk to me. Although, I can't imagine what you have to say to me. I don't even live here. I live in Yakima."

"He's trying to tell you that Catalin is dead, you idiot." Sheila finally found her voice, "But then I doubt you care about that anyway. You always hated her and now you can have all the money from the estate. I'm sure you're delighted."

"Dead? Is that true?" Joseba turned to Jonathon.

"Yes, I'm afraid it is. It appears that she was accidentally killed by a llama."

"By a llama? You've got to be joking. My sister was a damned dyke and impossible to get along with, but she was perfection itself when it came to animals. No way would she get in a position to be killed by a llama."

"Well, I'm sorry but all evidence points to her being knocked over by a llama and hitting her head on a metal tack box."

"Whatever, I really don't care how she died. Having her dead just means more work for me. I'm surprised that she managed to live as long as she did. Her whole lifestyle was a life of sin. It looks like the devil's claimed his own."

I looked over at Sheila. Her face was a mask of rage and agony. Her hands were balled into fists and I could tell that she was doing everything she could to keep from attacking the man.

"Jonathon, maybe you and Mr. Ezkarra could walk down to my booth to finish your business or into Rex's office."

"My business is finished here. The only reason I came was to get her to sign these papers. I have other things to do and no time to stand around talking."

"My impression from yesterday was that she didn't want to see you this weekend, Mr. Ezkarra," I said. "Why did you come today?"

"I came because I needed these damn papers signed and she was going to sign them or else. I don't have time to waste worrying about her sensibilities and schedules."

"Or else?" I asked. Catalin's brother started to step toward me when Jonathon broke in.

"I think we do still have business to take care of, Mr. Ezkarra. But if you are busy today, it can probably wait until later. Please give me your phone number so that I can contact you."

"Here's my card. Use my cell number as I won't be back in Yakima until Monday."

"OK, you'll be hearing from me. I'll talk to you later, Martha. If you two," Jonathon said, giving a nod in Ellen's direction, "come up with any bright ideas, I'll be back at the station."

"We'll let you know," I said, "but now we both have booths to tend to."

Before I left to go to my booth, I turned to Sheila. "I'm sorry you had to hear all of that. He's obviously an angry, misguided man."

"He's hated me for twenty years. It wasn't any different than I expected from him. But today, it was especially hard to take. Thanks for noticing and getting him moved out of here. Well, like you, I have work to do. It's going to be a long Gathering."

"Are you sure you want to stay?"

"I have to. This is my only income. I've been effectively a housewife for twenty years. Catalin pushed me out into the wide world a month ago, but the reality hadn't really set in until this morning. Up until then, I was sure we would overcome our problems. Now it's permanent and I didn't even get a chance to say good-bye."

Her eyes filled with tears. I would have liked to give her a hug but she radiated the need to keep her personal space. It was going to be hard for her for awhile.

"I'm sorry. I'll be here if you need anything this weekend, my booth is down next to the Pyr booth and the side door."

"I may be down later to talk to the Pyr people. I'm not sure what will happen to ours. I mean to Catalin's. I mean. Oh hell, I don't know what I mean. There are animals galore on that ranch that need to be taken care of and I'm sitting here not even knowing who they belong to. I guess I need an attorney."

"That might not be a bad idea. Why don't you talk to David Swanson? He's an excellent one and a good friend."

"That makes sense. Actually he's who Catalin used. I've met him. I guess I will give him a call after the Gathering."

"What's happening to the animals right now?" I asked.

"Rex said he'd send someone over to the ranch. I'm assuming that he has. In spite of recent events, he has been a good friend over the years."

"Good. Well, yell if you need anything."

I turned and walked down the line of vendors to my booth. The crowd was building and I was probably losing business by taking the time to talk to Sheila but she obviously was in distress.

"I wondered if you were going to work today," Ellen said as I walked up.

"Figured I'd better do something. I too have to eat, and this weekend is usually good for me."

"You'll find money in your cash box and a note as to what I've sold. You'd better get spinning if the early sales are any indication. Your handspun's going fast."

"Good. It has the largest margin of profit. I have more back at the shop that I can bring in later if I need to."

The next hour went by quickly as customers came and went. When I wasn't busy with my booth, I talked Pyrs with people who came by to see the big white dogs. We had a good mix of volunteers today in that booth. There were two people who had them as companion dogs and Ellen and I who used them as working dogs. That meant we could answer questions from all sides.

Unlike the shepherds, who did sell livestock, we never sold puppies at the Gathering. We did hand out the names of breeders, but our booth was informational only. That stopped any chance of an impulse purchase of a puppy. Pyr puppies are delightful but they grow into very big dogs who are independent, need to be fenced, and shed and bark a lot. It is not an acquisition that one wants to make lightly. Good breeders are very careful as to where they place their puppies. Education is what the Pyr booth is all about.

I'd just finished selling some silk roving and was talking to the customer when I felt an arm slip around my waist. I looked up to see Mark smiling down at me. I noticed that he was using the handspun braid that I'd made for him to hold his long black hair into a traditional Navajo bun at the nape of his neck. He was a slim six feet and all muscle. His black eyes were bright accents for his chiseled features. He was all that causes many to call the Diné a beautiful people.

"Hello, you. Do you know Michael Green? He was in my spinning class in February and usually shows up with the Ewe-phoric gang." There's a group of fiber people who come to the shop on Thursdays for a couple of hours to spin, knit, and enjoy each other's company. " He's decided to try his hand at spinning silk. He also teaches biology at Evergreen."

"Yes, Michael's the proud owner of a very large yellow tabby cat named Tigger. It's good to see you away from business, Michael. I hope Tigger is doing well."

"Tigger's doing fine, and it's good to see you too. Well, I need to see where else I can drop money here. Thanks for re-minding me of the Gathering when I was in the shop last week, Martha; otherwise, I would have forgotten it."

"I'm glad you're enjoying it. If you have time, go over and watch some of the fleece judging. I've learned a huge amount from watching them handle the fleece and listening to the comments. This year's judge is especially good at teaching while she does her job."

"I just may do that. I have no classes today so I'm free to do as I please. Might drop back by on my way out."

"OK, have a great time."

"You here for the llama?" I asked as I turned toward Mark.

"Yep, Jonathon said that you'd show me where he is. I also need to find James Diegos and get him to sign the paperwork that lets me drive off with his animal."

"Well, Pedro's over here. My guess is that we'll find James fairly close by. I think he has three other llama housed in the same area. I'll walk over with you because I need to check on Joseph and Juan and let Falcor out for awhile." I glanced at Ellen and she nodded saying that she'd watch over the booth again for me.

"Falcor came with you today?"

"He did and he was actually the reason that we checked Pedro's stall. He was not happy with the sounds coming from it. Once there, he also did an excellent job of keeping everyone out of the stall. He wouldn't even let Jonathon in until I told him it was OK."

We arrived at the stall that housed Pedro just as I finished talking and I heard a low woof from the adjoining stall as Falcor let me know that he'd heard me. Pedro had settled down from his earlier excitement and was resting at the back of the stall with the sheep clustered near him. He seemed totally at ease.

"I don't understand Jonathan's thinking. How could that animal have killed Catalin?" I said as we stood looking at him.

"I agree with you completely." I turned to see that the speaker was James.

"Hello, James," Mark said. "I've come to take Pedro with me."

"I don't like it, not at all. But if he has to go off, I'm glad it's with you, Mark. I know you'll take care of him."

"Absolutely. Well, let's go in and take a look at him. I'd like to check him over and see if we can find anything that might explain an attack."

The men opened the stall door and went in with Pedro. I moved to the adjacent stall and went in with my animals. Juan and Joseph appeared to be doing fine. They looked up and greeted me with their soft humming noises.

"Hey, pretty boys, how're you doing?"

Alpaca generally do not like to be handled. Often people look at these small camelids and think fuzzy, cute, soft animals that can be cuddled like you would a large fluffy dog. But these are not dogs or similar domesticated animals, and with young cria, you can set yourself up for disaster later. Cria who are bottlefed and generally handled heavily and played with can develop Aberrant Behavior Syndrome as they mature. This results in an animal that is nearly impossible to handle and dangerous to be around. It's an especially sad cause of animals ending up in rescue—or worse, euthanized—because it is avoidable if owners just do their home-work before they start raising or breeding alpaca or llamas. That being said, my two did enjoy a limited amount of touch from me and came over to get a few scratches behind their ears and to search my pocket to see if it held any treats. But they too avoided contact with other people. They weren't even fond of Ellen.

Falcor stood up and wandered over. He sniffed at Juan and then walked toward the stall door.

"You ready to get out of here?" My answer was a look back over his shoulder that said "Would I be standing here if I weren't?"

I grabbed his leash from where I'd draped it over the side of the stall earlier and hooked it to his collar.

"OK, let's go. You two behave yourselves," I said to the al-paca as Falcor and I exited the stall. I could still hear the men talking quietly in the stall next to me.

"I'm taking Falcor outside."

"We'll be out there with Pedro in a couple of minutes," Mark answered.

Falcor and I started down the row of stalls. When we came to Pedro's old stall, I noticed that it was marked off and people seemed to be avoiding it like it contained something contagious. That was probably just as well. From there I could continue down the stalls to the outside, through a side door on the parking lot side, or go through a large opening into the main arena and across to the door that was next to the Pyr booth. That door led out to the graveled area between the arena and the stables. I hadn't realized that the stall was so accessible during all the ruckus this morning. I was surprised that no one had seen anything before I got there. The sheep people were usually in the arena very early—much earlier than when I arrived. I suppose they were just focused on their own animals. Still, it made me wonder. Falcor and I opted for the closer door to the graveled parking lot. Going across the arena would have taken a whole lot longer since people always wanted to stop Falcor and comment on his size and beauty.

The day had turned as beautiful as the early morning sky had promised. The lovely warm sun seemed to belie in some way the tragedy that had greeted us on entering the arena this morning. It would have been nice to have just stayed outside and enjoyed it for awhile. But duty called, and it didn't take Falcor long to complete his business. We were soon turning back in to the building. We were ready to turn in to the arena when Mark approached with Pedro from the other direction. I didn't see James with him.

"No James?"

"He said he didn't want to go with me. He's quite upset at being separated from the llama. I gather that Pedro was his first and holds a very special place for James. Even though he knows I'll take good care of him, he's not happy about letting him go. He signed the paperwork at the stall and said he'd come by my stable tomorrow to see him."

"Now that you've seen him, can you imagine him being dangerous?"

"No, I can't. I agree with you, Jonathon needs to look further for his murderer."

"Now I just have to figure out a way to convince Jonathon of that. He can be pretty set in his ways when he wants to."

"I think you could let someone else convince him of it. I almost lost a favorite patient and could have lost you the last time you decided you didn't like Jonathon's solution to a murder."

"You couldn't have lost me then," I said with a grin. "You didn't have even a niggling of a claim on me at that time."

"Hmm, but I was working up to it. And if things had worked out differently, I'd have never had a chance."

"Well, I won't do anything crazy, but I'm going to keep my eyes and ears open."

I'd stopped because we'd crossed the arena and come parallel with the Pyr booth. It was time that I paid attention to mine. I could see Ellen looking over at me and rolling her eyes. That probably meant that she'd been forced into selling fiber again.

"What's that dangerous creature doing here? Why haven't you shot it? It's crazed."

A very upset, rather small young man barreled up to Mark and me. Pedro shied back and to the side. His eyes rolled and his humming started. He was distressed once again from the actions of this impetuous person.

"Whoa," Mark said, gentling Pedro and getting him back under control.

"How can you have that monster out here? He shouldn't be near people. He could kill again." The young man continued and I noticed that Falcor had quietly placed himself between me and the stranger. He didn't like the shouting and yelling either.

"He isn't a monster," I said. "He's actually quite gentle."

"Then why's he looking at me that way?" I looked over toward Pedro and saw that his ears were pressed back and his neck erect. He had moved into a more aggressive stance. But I would too if I had this creature yelling at me.

"Maybe because you've come at him aggressively. I might go on the defensive too if you came at me shouting, yelling and waving your arms."

"I'd suggest you back off a bit," Mark commented. "Give him some space and lower your tone of voice."

The young man did as he was told. He looked a little familiar although I couldn't place a reason why I might know him. Once he was back a few feet, Mark once again got Pedro so that he was comfortable.

"Now to answer your question," Mark said. "This animal isn't dangerous. He's suspected of an attack this morning but that hasn't been proven. For now the law says that he's to be quarantined and that's what will happen. So if you'll let me pass, I'll take him out of here as you suggest and get him into my trailer and taken to quarantine."

The young man looked like he wanted to respond but stood aside, and Mark passed with Pedro. As he headed out the door, he turned toward me.

"I'll talk to you later, Martha. Let me know if you hear anything before I do."

"I will. Take good care of that big boy. Now," I said as I turned to the young man and started moving toward my booth, "who are you?"

"I'm Kelmen Ezkarra." he said as he fell in step with me. Ahh, I now realized why he was familiar. He looked like a slight version of his father. For I was sure that this was

Catalin's nephew. I mean, how many Ezkarras could there be out there?

"I'm sorry, Kelmen. I can understand why you're distraught. The death of your aunt must have come as an awful shock."

"I didn't even know it had happened. I'd come to meet up with her and see the new lambs that she had for sale. She was really proud of those lambs. I'd just gotten out of my car when some woman wanted to know how I was doing. When I said I was doing fine, she said that I was a great specimen of a nephew. A few hours after a llama had killed my aunt, I was doing just fine. When I said that I didn't know, the woman proceeded to describe in detail the events of the morning. Then I walk into the building and I see this large llama walking toward me. I just lost it."

His eyes misted over and he turned away from me while making a swipe at his cheeks with his hand. I was sure he didn't want me to see him cry so I moved into my booth and started straightening some of the items on my front table.

"Were you and your aunt close?" I asked.

"She was the best. Oh, I know that she could drive people crazy but she was the most marvelous rancher. Her animals were beautiful and so well taken care of. I loved to go visit in the summer when I was a kid. I'd get to ride the horses and help her with the lambs. Some years I managed to wrangle the chance to come over during shearing season and help with the shearing. We talked about me joining her on the ranch when I finished my education. I'm going to Puget Sound Community College but I plan on transferring to Washington State to get my degree in animal husbandry. Now all of that looks like it's over."

"It sounds like she was a very special person for you. I'm sure she would want you to continue your education. It would be a tribute to her to go on and get your degree and continue in her chosen profession."

"You don't understand. She was helping me. My father would rather shoot me than see me become a shepherd. He says our people have risen above that. We need to move into more meaningful professions. He won't help with my school expenses at all. Aunt Catalin was the one who helped with that. Now she's gone. My dad'll be trying to haul me back to Yakima to work with him in that damn accounting firm. That and attending mass every time I turn around. I tell you, he'll do anything he can to make me miserable. Aunt Catalin was my escape. Now she's gone."

With that he gave me a look of distress, turned and walked out the door closest to us.

"He's one miserable young man," Ellen said. I had noticed that she was listening to us but hadn't drawn Kelmen's attention to it.

"Yes, he is," I said.

Chapter 6

Y ou want this big guy over with you to work the booth for awhile?" I asked Ellen. "You seem to be a bit low on big, white dogs."

"I'd appreciate it. Frosty is beginning to tire and our other help for this slot hasn't shown yet. Come on, Falcor. You can be a petting puppy for awhile."

I handed Falcor to Ellen and turned to the woman who was waiting patiently by one of my spinning wheels.

"Can I try spinning on this?" she asked in a voice gentle and low. Her gray hair was cut in a short bob and, although my height, she probably outweighed me by about thirty pounds. Her teal slacks and striped tee shirt were just a smidgen too tight, which made me wonder if the weight was a fairly recent addition.

"Of course, you can. Use some of the roving in the basket next to it."

"I've never used a double treadle before and this drive system seems different than the one in the class that I took years ago."

"This is a Scotch tension. It uses a brake band to set the tension for the bobbin. It's easy to use. Has it been quite awhile since you've done any spinning?"

"Yes, a number of years, but I decided this year that I was going to do it again. I just had the one class and then we moved and I never got back to it."

"Do you live near here?"

"Yes, I'm in Elma."

"Well, I periodically teach a class at my shop and we will be starting one on spinning with the wheel the first of June if you're interested. It will be on Thursday evenings. However, for now, let's see if we can get you started on this machine. I'll demonstrate just a little bit for you and then you can try."

I pulled a chair up to the wheel.

"This wheel is an Ashford Joy. It's one of the most portable of all the spinning wheels. It's small enough when folded to fit in an overhead bin on an airplane. As you noticed, this model is a double treadle but it is also available in a single treadle."

While I was talking, I drafted a piece of roving out to a thickness that was just a little bit thicker than what I wanted my yarn to be and hooked it to the leader on the bobbin.

"You just want to keep your rhythm even as you use both treadles. Don't try to treadle too fast. It isn't necessary. Then draft your yarn out with your dominant hand and use your other hand to control the twist. One of the nice things about the Joy is the orifice is in the center so it doesn't matter which hand you use to draft."

"It looks familiar. I think I'm ready to try it."

I moved out of the chair and handed the piece of roving to her after she was seated.

"OK, now start treadling slowly. That's it. You don't have to use speed, especially when you are just getting the hang of it."

"Oops, now what do I do?" She had let her roving separate and lost the yarn onto the bobbin.

"We just pull it back out and re-thread it," I said as I looped the yarn over the appropriate hook on the flyer and then used the orifice hook to get the yarn back through the orifice. I pulled out enough yarn so that she had about a foot to work with.

"Now fringe out the end of the yarn and place it horizontally across your roving. Treadle very slowly and let the yarn catch the fibers of the roving. That's it. Now as you continue to treadle slowly, pinch off just above your roving with your left hand and draft out some more fiber with your right. That's good. Now pinch with your right hand just above the fiber and release the twist by letting up on the pinch at your left hand. The twist will go into your drafted fiber and you can allow your yarn to pull onto the bobbin."

I watched as she carefully followed my instructions. I could see that her hands were beginning to remember the earlier training they had received. Muscle memory is an amazing thing. "You've got it. Now you just keep repeating that operation."

"This is fun," she said after working with it for a few minutes. "I think I would like to buy a wheel, but I'm not sure I want to today."

"That's quite all right. I'll give you my card. Why don't you come by the shop in the next week or so. You can try again and sample some of the other wheels. You can also sign up for the spinning class if you want to."

"I think I'll do just that. I'd like to see some additional wheels and I do want to take the class. If I'm going to purchase the wheel, I might as well learn how to do things right."

"I'm Martha Williamson," I said as I gave her my card.

"Thank you. I'm Gloria McKenna, and I'll probably come by next week. It should be great fun. Oh, and who are you?"

I glanced over to where she was looking and could see Falcor looking into the booth, making sure all was in order here.

"That's Falcor. He's one of my two livestock guardian dogs."

"He's beautiful. Is he gentle?"

"As long as neither I nor his flock are in danger, yes. He is very protective and will use the measure of force necessary to see that we do not get into trouble."

"Well, he's gorgeous. I hope that I'll see more of him if I come visit you."

"You will, as well as his helper, Denali."

"Goodbye, Falcor. I'll see you next week too." With that she moved on down to the next vendor and Falcor turned his attention to a young child who had just grabbed his ruff from behind. I was glad that he was as gentle and patient as he was, but I did wish that people would train their children better on handling a strange dog. Just as I was thinking of commenting, Ellen stepped in to explain how a dog should be approached.

I glanced at my watch. It was well past lunch time and my stomach was beginning to make some complaints. The crowd had dissipated again from the Pyr booth.

"I'll get us some lunch, if you want to keep an eye out here."

"Can do. What do you have in mind?"

"Don't know. I'll go see who has food booths set up."

"OK. Just add in something cold to drink. I'm very tired of coffee and I forgot to put in any water for me."

"Will do," I said as I headed out the door into the bright sunshine.

"Do you know where the Spinning for Socks class is being held?"

I turned to see a young woman dressed in jeans and last year's Fiber Gathering sweatshirt rapidly walking toward me. Her long brown hair was caught up rather haphazardly into a bun on the top of her head and there were tendrils falling down the back of her neck and around her face, which was brightened by a smile that filled her eyes and crinkled the area around her mouth. She was holding multiple bags, including a tote bag that had knitting needles poking out of the top. Obviously she had made some vendors happy.

"The classes are held in two rooms that are at the very end of the building. You reach them from the outside so just keep walking in the direction you're going and then turn right when you get to the end. I'm sure they'll have the doors marked as to which class is in which room."

"Thank you," she said as she collapsed on one of the benches next to a picnic table. "I spent so much time shopping that I thought I was going to be late, but I think I have time for a moment's breather. My name is Joy."

I smiled. The name seemed to fit her. "I'm Martha Williamson."

"You aren't laden with bags. Don't tell me that you've resisted all the wonderful goodies in there."

"I have so far, but I'll probably succumb at some point. I have one of the booths, The Spider's Web."

"Oh, you must be further down the row. I think I only got halfway through when I decided that I needed to find my class. I'm so excited about it. I love knitting socks and I've been spinning for awhile now. I can't wait to learn to make my own yarn for my socks."

"I'm sure it will be a great class. The teacher is one of the best in the country. I love taking classes from her."

"Oh, and I guess I'd better get down there or I will be late. It was nice to meet you, Martha. I'll be back tomorrow and be sure to stop by your booth."

"Enjoy your class, Joy. See you later."

I watched her as she headed toward her class. I bet she would be a delight for any teacher to have among their students. Then turning back to the food booths, I tried to make up my mind. The Boy Scout troop had burgers, chips, and soda. Sally's Black Hills Cafe had soups, salads, and various bread products, and the Black Hills High School Boosters were selling chili, which smelled wonderful. I walked up to their booth,

"Can I help you, Martha?" Bob Mitchell smiled at me from behind the booth counter.

"Hey, Bob, who's handling the station?" Bob owned the most popular service station in town,

"Jimmy Thomas. He started working for me about two months ago and is doing an excellent job. Figured I could trust him to handle things for my shift here. Now what can I get you to eat?"

"Two small bowls of chili, two small bags of corn chips and two bottles of water. I love corn chips in my chili. If Ellen doesn't, that just means more for me."

"Coming right up, and I can tell you that this is the best chili you could possibly find. Jonathon brought the recipe back with him from New Mexico. It's James Hernandez's recipe, and it has just the right balance of spice and hot."

"Great, I love good chili."

"Here you go. Let me know what you think of it."

"Will do," I said as I headed back to the booths where Ellen would be waiting not too patiently for the food.

Ellen and I had just finished our lunch and I'd disposed of the dishes when I looked down the line of vendors and blinked. I'd have sworn that the woman striding toward me managing to look regal in a caftan reminiscent of the '60s holding a well-filled matching tote bag was my aunt Margaret. But what was she doing here? She had a massive number of interests, but fiber crafts weren't among them as far as I knew. Was she keeping secrets from me? The woman drew near and I was correct. It was my aunt.

"Aunt Margaret, what are you doing here?"

"And I can't come check on my favorite niece?" Aunt Margaret's my height or slightly taller, and she keeps her full head of silver hair beautifully cut in a shoulder-length style that frames her face, and her hands are always well manicured. Today there was a glint in her eye and a total look of mischief on her face.

"Of course you can, but you've never done it before."

"Always a first time, but actually I was invited by a young friend of mine. Annela Wong is an author who writes mysteries that have a fiber theme and she was coming down to spend the afternoon doing research. She asked me to come along and I jumped at the opportunity since I knew you would be here."

"What, you know a mystery writer whose topic is fiber and you've never introduced me?" I said with a pout and my hands on my hips.

"She just moved into our building a few months ago and I've only recently become acquainted with her. But I'll make sure that you meet her today."

"OK, forgiven. So what do you think of the Gathering so far?"

"Well, I'm not ready to take up spinning and knitting as you would guess, but I did find some really nice things."

She promptly set her tote bag on my table and began to pull out all sorts of treasures. There was my favorite lanolin moisturizer, and a lovely woven scarf that appeared to be made of bamboo yarn.

Bamboo yarn is a form of rayon. Rayon can be made from many different plant materials, but one of the favorites among textile people in the last few years has been bamboo. Using a readily renewable plant source appeals to people and the end product is incredibly soft and has a sheen similar to silk. There are still ecological considerations because of the chemical and industrial process that it takes to produce it, but when compared to petroleum-based fibers like nylon and polyester, rayon gets my vote hands down.

She continued to delve into her bag and added a lovely shawl of soft wool in a gorgeous array of blues and greens to the growing pile on my table. She then finished it off with a felted wool bag in a wild color scheme of purples, pinks, reds and yellows that might look foolish used by some people, but not my aunt Margaret.

"Wow! You did make a bunch of fiber artists happy. Beautiful choices."

About that time, Falcor pushed forward from where he had been standing, politely waiting to be noticed. I guess he decided that he'd waited long enough.

"Hello, Falcor," Aunt Margaret said as she squatted down so she was at eye level with him and began scratching his ears and chest. "How has your day been? Exciting?"

"More exciting than I would have liked," I said, and proceeded to tell her about Falcor finding Catalin this morning.

"Not a good way to start a day," she responded as she stood up from that low position with grace and ease. There is something to be said for yoga practice to keep one supple into their early sixties.

"It wasn't, and I'm sure that it wasn't a simple accident either. But so far that is the official finding. She was accidentally killed by the llama in the stall where Falcor found her."

At that moment, a beautiful Eurasian woman in her mid-thirties, early forties walked up.

"Did you hear that, Annela? There may actually be a real murder mystery connected with the fiber festival."

"You're joking. Right?" she said, looking at my aunt to see if her face confirmed the statement.

"No, I'm not. My niece, Martha. Oh, by the way, Martha, this is Annela Wong. Annela, this is my favorite niece, Martha Williamson. Anyway, Martha and Falcor — that's him with all the fur and four feet looking at you — found a dead woman this morning when they got to the Festival."

"Is she correct?" Annela now looked at me and then at Falcor, who made a move toward her in order to be introduced but then returned to me when she stepped back and obviously didn't really want to say hello. I wondered if she was afraid of him or just not very interested and comfortable with dogs. It is the rare person who snubs Falcor.

"I'm afraid she is. However, at this point it has been ruled an accident, not a murder," I said as I gave my aunt a look that I hoped said she might have spoken out of turn.

"How tragic and interesting. Did Margaret tell you that I'm an author who writes cozy murder mysteries with a fiber theme?"

"She did, and I scolded her for keeping you a secret, but

she says that you haven't known each other long. I love cozy mysteries. Have you written many?"

"I have one published with It's a Crime Press. It's titled *Dyeing Is Deadly* and takes place at a dye workshop. The main character owns a mountain craft retreat in Colorado. I'm thinking of having her go to the Estes Park Wool Market in the next book so I wanted to get some firsthand experience with a fiber festival."

"You picked a good, small festival by coming here. You might also want to spend some time at Black Sheep Gathering in Eugene, Oregon, in June. It is the largest of the fiber festivals in the Pacific Northwest and always a packed weekend of classes, fleece judging, and lots of vendors."

"I'd heard about Black Sheep, but hadn't really checked it out. You think it's worth my time?"

"I do. I don't vend there because of the distance, but I love to attend it."

"I might have to go this year then. I'll have to see what June looks like on my schedule."

"Well, your book sounds like a lot of fun and it's definitely a theme I'm interested in. I'll have to get a copy. Is it available online?"

"Yes, it's at all the major online book retailers and many brick and mortar stores too. There's also a digital version available."

"Martha's done some sleuthing herself," Aunt Margaret said.

"You have?"

"Aunt Margaret's exaggerating," I said.

"She solved a murder and consequently freed an innocent man this past winter, no matter what she says," Aunt Margaret said with conviction.

"I think we might have a lot in common," Annela said with a smile. "Maybe we can get together and talk about it. Are you planning on coming to Seattle anytime soon."

"I'll be up there in two weeks to go to the theater with Aunt Margaret. Maybe we could get together the next day as I plan to spend the night."

"That sounds wonderful. Maybe for brunch. I'll set up the exact time with Margaret after I look at my calendar, but right now, Margaret, we really need to get heading back north. I have an appointment this evening."

Aunt Margaret gave both Falcor and me a hug and returned all her treasures to her tote bag. "OK, I'm ready."

"It was good to meet you, Martha. I look forward to seeing you soon."

"I'm glad to meet you too. I hope you got the information you needed from your visit today."

"I did, and maybe an idea of how my murder might happen in the next book."

"Great, I look forward to reading it. You can go out this side door if you want. It lets you avoid some of the crowd."

Aunt Margaret gave me another hug and followed Annela out the door. I noticed that she pointedly avoided the Pyrs next door while Aunt Margaret stopped to pet every one of them. Obviously, Annela was not a dog person.

Chapter 7

The rest of the afternoon went by quickly. I had excellent sales at my booth and would have to bring additional stock in tomorrow to replenish some areas. That was an advantage of living so close to the Gathering. Some of the vendors didn't have that option.

When I wasn't busy selling fiber, I helped out at the Pyr booth. The big white dogs acted like magnets and there was a constant stream of people stopping to pet them. Some of them were shepherds who were seriously interested in livestock guardians. However, most of them were members of the general public who were attracted by the presence of the dogs. A few might turn into Pyr owners at some time, but if we did our job correctly most would decide that other breeds were better for them. Livestock Guardian breeds, including the Great Pyrenees, had specific needs and were often not the best choice for a family companion.

Thursday was the early closing day for the Gathering and the five o'clock shutdown was rapidly approaching. We would be open until seven both Friday and Saturday and then on Sunday, we again closed at five.

I was just finishing a sale when Ellen wandered over.

"I've just taken a call from one of my clients and he wants me to meet him at the Sky Mountain Casino for dinner. Want to join us? Donovan won't mind."

"I'd love to if I can take Falcor home first and get a shower before we go. What time do you have to be there?"

"I told him I needed to do the same thing so we decided to meet at seven-thirty."

"OK, want to pick me up on your way out of town?"

"Can do."

Another customer wandered into my booth and people were gathering around Falcor again so we went back to our respective business. In no time, I heard the gong that signaled that the doors would be closing to the general public in five minutes. As I had no one in my booth and I needed to take care of Juan and Joseph for the evening, I pulled the sheets over my booth and pulled all but a starting bank out of my cash box.

"I'll take my dog now, lady," I said as I walked over to where Ellen was standing talking to one of the shepherds.

"Isn't that the dog that was guarding the stall this morning?"

"Yes, he is."

"He was superb. I had no desire to cross him. Is he that good when he's protecting his livestock?"

"He is. I've had no predator kills since he and Denali took on the job of watching over my critters. However, I have a very small operation. Ellen here has a somewhat larger one and she'll tell you the same thing. And if you want to know how they work in a large operation, you might talk to Sheila Barnes down at her booth. She and Catalin worked four pair."

"Four pair. That's a lot. I might just do that."

Taking Falcor's leash, I left Ellen to continue talking to him while I went over to take care of Juan and Joseph.

The alpaca were glad to see me and greeted me with their low humming. Falcor came into the stall with me and nuzzled them to let them know that all was fine. It didn't take me long to give them their grain for the evening and freshen their water.

I was about to leave when it dawned on me that I should maybe check on Catalin's sheep in the next booth. I wasn't sure if Sheila would remember them given her understandable emotional state. However, my worries were unfounded. Sheila or someone had made sure that they were well supplied with both food and water and their bedding straw had been freshened too. Once again I marveled at the lovely condition of Catalin's sheep. She'd obviously loved her animals and given them the best of care. What a loss to have her struck down at such an early age. I wondered as Sheila did who would end up with the animals. I hoped that it was Sheila.

Then looking at the animals, I had to wonder once again if they could also be the reason for Catalin's death. Had someone wanted her animals and ranch enough to kill her? Could it have been Sheila?

However, I wasn't going to answer those questions tonight. Since all was well here and my animals were settled, I gathered up Falcor and headed for the parking lot.

"Ok, big guy, up into your crate. We're going home. I'm sure that Denali will be very glad to see you."

Falcor responded at once and collapsed in his crate. Being a demo dog was exhausting work and he would sleep well tonight. However, I knew that even as tired as he was, he'd keep his ears open and be out into the fields immediately at the slightest sound of a coyote in the area.

Denali greeted us with multiple barks as I pulled into the driveway. I could tell that she was very much ready for Falcor to be home.

"Here he is, lady." I opened the gate and followed Falcor in. He and Nali sniffed each other to make sure all was well with their partner. Then Nali came over to me to get scratched. I turned and headed into the barn with the Pyrs following. It didn't take me long to make sure that everyone was fed, watered and bedded down for the night. Nali followed me back out to the gate when I was done. "You have to stay back here for awhile longer, big girl. I'm leaving for the evening and you're still on guard duty."

With that, I closed the gate again and went to get ready for dinner with Ellen and her client. I was beginning to wonder if I were nuts to be going out. It had been a more exhausting day than usual because of the trauma and excitement around Catalin's death and just working the booth on a normal day was tiring.

A shower helped a lot in reviving me. I decided on a long black denim skirt and a handknit cashmere sweater in a light green that brought out the green in my hazel eyes. Boots with a moderate heel and my squash blossom necklace and earrings finished off the outfit. I pulled my hair up into a French twist and fastened it with a hair pin of Navajo silver that Mark had given me for my birthday this past March. I smiled as I remembered that evening. We'd had a double celebration: my birthday and Denali's return to guard duty after her close brush with death. It was touch and go for awhile, but she's a strong- willed girl and she pulled through, much to the delight of the many of us who love her. I took one last look in the mirror and decided I was ready to go, which was good because I heard the alarm barks from the Pyrs and tires on the driveway.

I grabbed my jacket and went out to meet Ellen. It would be nice to have a good dinner that someone else cooked.

Chapter 8

H ey, lady, that's quite a transformation," Ellen said as I climbed into the car.

"Back at you, lady." Ellen was in an elegant red wool pantsuit with a cream silk blouse. Her hair was braided and then worked into an elaborate knot at the nape of her neck. I wondered how she managed it by herself. I'm much more of a klutz with my hair in spite of my ability with fiber that isn't attached to me.

We were soon on the highway and heading toward Elma. We exited the highway at Elma and continued along the Monte-Elma Road to Brady. When Ellen turned onto the Middle Satsop Road, I was glad she was driving. I hadn't a clue as to where the casino actually was. She was soon turning right onto a smaller paved road and shortly we were driving onto the casino property.

"Wow. I had no idea it was this large a complex," Ellen said.

We were looking at what might have been a college campus with three large cedar buildings connected to each other by covered, glassed-in walkways. The Satsop River flowed to the rear of the manicured lawn and gardens, and its song added to the ambience of the place.

"Neither did I. I wonder where the best spot would be to park," I said as I looked at multiple-story parking garages and additional lots, all of which seemed to be quite full.

"I think I'll opt for the valet parking. This is a business meeting so I can take it off as an expense. I have no real desire to try to find a parking spot."

"Sounds good to me. This place is really hopping and it isn't even the weekend yet."

Ellen pulled up and handed her car over to the young man at the valet desk, who looked appreciatively at the red Lexus SUV my friend drives. Ellen has a small trust fund from her grandmother that lets her spoil herself in some ways, and her car is one way she does that.

"Donovan said to meet him in the River Wind building. I think it's this one on the left," Ellen said.

We walked through the doors into an elegant space. Huge windows looked out onto the gardens in the back of the building and onto the driveway in the front. The upper walls, beams and ceiling were of rough hewn cedar and the lower walls and huge fireplace were of natural stone. What looked like original artwork hung on the walls and two large masks guarded either side of the fireplace. Ellen looked around for her client. It took a minute. Then she spotted him on the other side of the fireplace. Just at that moment, he looked up and waved. He was tall, dark and heavily built without being fat. His long hair was pulled back into a pony tail, with what looked like a band of

Hawaiian feather work holding it in place, and his black eyes seemed to take in everything around him with interest.

"Thanks for meeting with me tonight," he said as he walked up and gave Ellen a hug.

"Martha, this is Donovan Keawe. Donovan, this is Martha Williamson. Martha is a good friend who I thought might help us brainstorm tonight. She just didn't know that she was being invited to work."

"Good to meet you, Martha."

"And you, Donovan. Are you Hawaiian?"

"Yes, I am. How'd you know?"

"The last name was a pretty good giveaway plus they're the only people I know who regularly hug people they've just met." He grinned with that last statement as I continued. "I was born in Honolulu, but my real experience with Hawai`i was when my husband and I were stationed there for four years. It's a beautiful state."

"That it is. I come from the Hilo side of Hawai`i."

"I've never been to the Big Island. But I'll get there one day. It's on my short list of vacation spots."

"Your Hawai`i experience is one reason I asked you here tonight, Martha. Donovan is setting up a Web site dedicated to Hawaiian music and I thought you might give us your perspective from both the outlook of a mainlander and someone who's lived in the islands."

"Well, I'm not sure how much help I'll be, but I'm willing."

"I knew you would be. Now where is that restaurant, Donovan? I'm starved and I'm sure Martha is too. Lunch at the Fiber Gathering was quite awhile ago."

"Right this way, ladies. We're going to eat at the River Grill tonight. I've found their food to be exceptional on a regular basis."

Donovan led the way, and we were soon seated at a corner table that looked through more massive windows onto the lovely gardens. There was a large fountain off to the right on the outside patio. It featured a magnificent sculpture of an eagle fishing and some salmon working their way upstream.

"This meal's on me," Donovan said, "so order whatever you want. Me, I'm going for the biggest steak they have."

"They have fresh halibut, so that's my choice," I said.

"Make that two of us," Ellen added.

When we'd placed our orders, including a calamari appetizer and a bottle of a dry Oregon Gewürztraminer, I turned to Donavan.

"I've been in a few casinos, and they were never totally pleasant experiences because of the heavy level of smoke in them. But this one seems to be smoke free. How do they manage it?"

Donovan smiled. "You noticed. That's one reason I come here even though it is a bit out of the way. It's also why there are multiple buildings to the complex. The River Wind building is totally smoke free in all of the rooms. They even have a small gambling area with slot machines and one blackjack table here that is smoke free. Although you do have to brave the smoke if you want roulette, poker or some of the more elaborate slots. I'll take you over there before you leave just so you can get a feel for it."

"Thanks, I'd like that, but I'm glad that our dinner is in a smoke-free area."

At that moment our calamari and wine were delivered, and our conversation turned to Ellen's design for the Web site.

"You know," I said, "many mainlanders are not familiar with Hawaiian music, but if they know anyone, it'll be Brother Iz. I'd feature him right up front. Then you can lead them into the wealth of other music by Hawaiian performers that is out there."

"I think I agree with you, Martha," Donovan said. "Iz was a wonderful ambassador for Hawaiian music. Then, Ellen, I think we need to have different pages for the various genres of the music. Does that make sense to you?"

"It does. Do you have permission to use CD labels or pictures of the artists?"

"I do for some of them. I will need to get it for others."

"I hope," I interjected, "that you will have some of the current, young musicians such as Makana featured too."

"I love Makana, Martha, and I agree that we need a section for the musicians coming up along with the classics. Taking notes, Ellen?"

"I am. I knew there was a reason I brought Martha."

At that point, our food was delivered and we wandered into other areas of conversation. It turned out that Donovan had been here in Washington for just about the same amount of time as I had – five years. We had fun talking about different areas in Hawai`i. After dinner, Donovan and Ellen wrapped up their business quickly and we were soon ready to leave.

"OK, Donovan," Ellen said, "how about that tour through the main casino, so we can figure out what all the excitement is about."

"Sounds good," I said. "I've never understood the draw, but then, Vegas never called to me either, in spite of it being the top vacation spot for people from Hawai`i."

"I must admit that I do enjoy the blackjack tables from time to time," Donovan said. "Come on and I'll lead the way. I've spent some enjoyable hours here and have to say probably left more money than I've won. Nothing major, though. However,

I'm afraid some people do go into this way beyond their means. It's sad to see that when it happens."

Donovan led us back through the beautiful lobby with its northwest motif and down a short hall to a set of double glass doors. These led to a covered walkway that was banked on one side by the now ubiquitous windows looking out over the entrance and parking area and on the other side by windows looking out over the gardens. At the end of the walkway, we went through another set of double doors and into another short hall that led into the gaming area of the resort. I couldn't believe the size of the place. They seemed to have tables for every game of chance one could want and slots and more slots. People were everywhere and most of them were smoking. Given that, I was actually amazed that the air wasn't more thoroughly filled with smoke. They must have one major air flow system. This was obviously a very popular spot and I guess if I were really into gambling, I could handle the level of smoke that was here. However, I think I'd find myself content with what was offered in the smoke-free environment. I looked around and didn't see any poker tables. That seemed odd since it's so popular right now.

"Don't they offer poker here?" I asked, turning to Donovan.

"They sure do and some of the games can run to pretty high stakes. As a matter of fact, on Thursdays they have a no-limit game. Poker is played in a private room down this way. You want to play? It's on our way out." he asked with a grin.

"Not this girl. I have no knowledge of poker. It's surprising how many people think they do and then lose their shirt. In a place like this, I'm sure it's not a game for the novice."

Just as we found ourselves outside the poker room, the door opened. I was surprised when I thought I recognized the young man who walked out. It was Kelmen Ezkarra and he didn't look happy. What was he doing here? Wasn't it just this morning that he was telling me that he didn't have enough money for school? I started to hail him and then thought better of it. He didn't see me because I was blocked by Donovan and he was moving fast.

"Did you see that?" I asked Ellen.

"See what?"

"Kelmen Ezkarra just walked out of that door."

"You're kidding. What would a broke college kid be doing in a high-stakes poker game?"

"I was thinking the same thing. I suppose there are those in the area who would lend money, but you'd think that they would want some chance of getting it back. Kelmen didn't appear to be a very good loan prospect, and borrowing money for gambling is truly foolhardy."

"If you're addicted to gambling," Donovan said, "common sense doesn't enter in. I had a college roommate who ended up in jail when his gambling addiction led to robbery."

I looked at Ellen and she said what I was thinking. "I wonder if it could lead to murder."

"Murder?" Donovan asked.

"Kelmen's aunt was killed sometime between yesterday evening and early this morning," I answered. "The jury is still out as to whether it was a terrible accident or murder, but Ellen and I are leaning in the direction of murder."

"Seems like a casino is an odd place to be right after your aunt is murdered whether you're guilty or not," Donovan said. "I know I wouldn't be anywhere but with my family if my auntie were killed."

"I think the family is pretty dysfunctional, but I agree with you, Donovan; a casino doesn't quite seem like the place for a grieving nephew to be spending his evening."

We had continued down the hall during our conversation and were once again at a set of double doors. These gave us a choice of going into a hallway that led to a third building or out into the night. We moved outside and onto the sidewalk in front of the complex.

"Can I buy you both a nightcap?" Donovan asked. "The bar in the River Wind building is really quite lovely."

"I don't think so," Ellen answered. "We have to be up quite early to get back to the Fiber Gathering. Maybe next time. I will get started on your Web page design, though, and I should have some examples for you to see by the middle of next week."

"Great. I'll look forward to your call."

"Thanks for a lovely dinner, Donovan," I said, "and it was great to meet you. Maybe next time we can talk more about Hawai`i and the Big Island. I would love to visit there some day."

"I'd like that, Martha. Have Ellen bring you along next time and we'll plan some time to talk story, too."

"I'll do that," Ellen answered. "Talk to you soon."

It was quite cool and clear as we walked down the sidewalk toward the valet parking desk. I'm sure the stars were bright but all the ambient light from the resort made it hard to see them. When we got to the front of the River Wind building, Ellen asked the valet to get her car and we waited in comfortable silence for it to arrive.

"I liked Donovan," I said as Ellen turned onto Middle Satsop Road. "How did you meet him?"

"He saw some work I had done for another client and called me. We have talked on the phone a couple of times but this was the first time that I'd seen him. I agree; I liked him too. I think it should be a fun assignment. How early do you plan to be there tomorrow?"

"We don't open until nine o'clock, but I'll probably be there no later than eight o'clock so I can take care of the alpaca and get my booth restocked and cleaned up a little."

"I'll probably be there after nine o'clock. I don't have to open up tomorrow, and I have a lot of work to do at home. Are you bringing Falcor with you?"

"No, I'll bring Denali. It is stressful being at the show, so I figured that I would give him a rest. Also, Denali actually enjoys the people contact more than Falcor does."

"I may bring Shasta in tomorrow. She isn't that much help for Tahoma yet and the socializing would be good for her."

We continued the ride back to Black Hills chatting about gossip around town and the fact that it was very odd to see Kelmen at the casino. As Ellen turned into my driveway, we were, as usual, greeted by the deep barks of Nali and Falcor.

"Looks like they're on duty," Ellen said.

"Yep, and I like it that way. Well, I'll see you tomorrow."

"Will do. I'll get the gate when I go out."

"Thanks." I gave Ellen a hug and climbed out of the car. It had been a lovely evening but I was more than ready to head for bed.

Chapter 9

Hello, pretty girl," Rex said to Nali as we walked into the arena Friday morning. "I don't think you'll find the excitement that your buddy found yesterday."

"I sure hope not," I said. "I'd have preferred less excitement then too."

"That makes two of us. Sheila stayed and talked to me for a long time last night. She was very worried about the animals. I assured her that I had people taking care of them, and she needn't worry. She was horribly hurt when Catalin kicked her out. I still have no idea why it happened. Sheila wouldn't talk about it; she just said that there was a terrible misunderstanding. I do wonder though if the loss of everything that she had worked for over twenty years could push her off the edge. Grief and money do funny things to people."

"She was very angry when Catalin brought this particular batch of lambs in on Wednesday," I said. "She said that they were hers and not Catalin's to sell. They had a fight just as Ellen and I were leaving for the night. Both were furious. Sheila did threaten to get her lambs back, but I figured it was just anger talking. I think I still feel that way. Under all the angry words, it felt like these were two people who still loved each other very much."

"I feel that way too," Rex said, "but I wonder if she will inherit the ranch."

"I guess that will come out over the next few days. It could make a difference. But then, would she know that she was going to inherit?"

"She'd probably know what the will said before Catalin kicked her out. I guess it would depend on whether Catalin had changed it yet. It's a very big and profitable spread," Rex added. "It might be worth killing for if you were that type of person."

"I don't feel that Sheila is, but who knows. Well, I need to take care of my alpaca and get my booth set up. I'll see you around later, Rex."

I decided to walk past Catalin's lovely ewe and the stalls that held her rams and lambs on the way to Juan and Joseph. I noticed that someone had already taken care of them, so evidently Sheila was here early this morning. I needed to give her a card and ask her to contact me when everything had sorted itself out. I still thought I'd like one of these lambs.

Nali's head went up and she sniffed the air when we got close to our guys. As soon as I opened the gate, she was inside checking them out. "Are they all right, big girl?"

She turned and gave me a quizzical look that asked why they were here and not home where they belonged. She then gave them another sniff and went over to a corner, circled a couple of times and lay down.

I pulled a couple of baby carrots out of my pocket as the alpaca came over to check me out. My guys love treats, and I felt they'd earned them by putting up with being here. I gave them each a pat and a look over for any problems. All seemed to be fine. After cleaning their stall and putting fresh straw down, it was time to feed and water them and head for my booth.

"You staying here or coming with me, Nali?" She answered by getting up and walking to the gate. "OK, you can come back to rest later in the morning."

I checked once more to make sure that the gate to the stall was locked and the "Do Not Pet" sign was still in place, then Nali and I made our way over to my booth. It took awhile because everyone wanted to stop and talk to the pretty dog. There was no one at the Pyr booth yet, so I took advantage of their absence and put Nali in one of their crates. I needed to go back out to the van and get the supplies I had brought to restock parts of my booth.

I walked past the fleece judging area. They were pulling the natural-colored Romney and getting them organized for the judging. I wished I had time to sit and watch. The year before I opened my shop, I spent a lot of time watching the judging here and again at Black Sheep Gathering in Oregon later in the year. I learned a lot about fleece from both experiences. I encouraged all my students and friends who were into fiber to take the time to watch. I would be purchasing some fleece when they went on sale tomorrow, but today all I had time for was a cursory look as I hurried out to the van.

We were having another beautiful spring morning. There were barn swallows swooping and diving around the buildings looking for any insects that were silly enough to fly within their reach. I love the graceful birds and they are marvels at keeping flying pests at bay. I know that some people find them messy and don't like them around, but I put up with their mess to have the joy of watching them and their constant help with the mosquito patrol.

I soon had my dolly loaded with the boxes of handspun, spindles and pattern books that I had brought to replenish the booth. Not only my handspun but also the spindles out of Hawaiian woods had sold out yesterday. It was always interesting to see what the hot item would be each year. Last year it was anything that had to do with silk. You can never tell. You just hope that you have the right items stocked when everything starts.

I went by Sheila's booth on my way back in but she wasn't there yet. I also stopped and bought my year's supply of lanolin hand cream. There was a vendor here each year who sold the best hand and face cream available. I always buy enough to get me through to the next year. We took a few minutes to chat about the crowd and our experience the day before. She also wanted to know about Catalin's death. I could only tell her what I'd found and Jonathon's official take on it. She seemed to accept that as plausible. I suppose it was, but I still had trouble thinking that the gentle llama that I met would attack anyone. And from our conversation first thing this morning, Rex was having problems with it too.

The Pyr booth was being set up by the time I got back, so I took Nali out of their crate and over to be with me. They had two adults and a puppy to start out with so they didn't need her, and she would enjoy visiting with the people in my booth. I had just finished putting the last supplies out when I heard the gong signaling the official start of the day. Of course, some sales had been going on prior to this as vendors bought from each other and a few people came through the doors early. None of us turned down a sale just because it was earlier than the official start time.

"This is dog hair?" A short, rather stout, young woman with a quizzical smile and a nose that seemed just a little too large for her round face was holding one of my skeins of handspun.

"It's fifty percent dog hair from my Great Pyrenees. The other fifty percent is merino wool."

"I can't believe how soft it is and it doesn't smell like dog hair at all. Could it be used for a hat for my daughter?"

"Yes. It would have to be hand washed, but there is no reason why you couldn't create a hat for her out of it. It will be incredibly warm so you might want to knit a size big enough to fit her next winter. Dog hair yarn gets a bloom just like angora does so you will want to take that into consideration when you're choosing a pattern."

"I really like this. Do you like it, sweetie?" she asked the baby in the stroller she was pushing. The little one looked to be about nine months old and was busy looking all around at the various sights and sounds.

I blanched a bit as she put it in reach of the child who had a chocolate cookie in her hand. But she just brushed it along the child's cheek. The baby gurgled, which I supposed was a positive response.

"She likes it, so I'll take it." She handed me the yarn with her money.

"Is there anything else I can get you? Would you like to look at the pattern books?"

"No, I don't — oh my gosh what is that?"

I turned to see what she was looking at and realized that Denali had gotten up from where she was sleeping.

"That is Nali, the dog that provided the hair for your yarn," I said with a chuckle.

"She's huge. What kind is she?"

"She's a Great Pyrenees and she guards my livestock when she's at home. Right now her partner, Falcor, has solo duty with that job."

"Can I pet her? Will she hurt the baby?"

"Yes to your first question and no to the second." I turned to Nali. "Come over here, big girl. These people want to meet you."

Nali wandered over and let herself be petted by the young woman and have her fur pulled by the baby. She then looked at me as if to say, "Want to get me out of this?" I picked up the woman's package and change.

"Here is your yarn. Is there anything else you'd like to see?"

"I don't think so. I guess we should be going. It was nice meeting you, Nali."

She gave Nali one last pat, released her fur from the baby's grasp and had started down the line of vendors when she realized that there were more Pyrs next to me. As I turned my attention to another customer and Nali went back to her corner, I heard her asking the Pyr booth about the dogs.

The early morning went by quickly and soon I looked up to see Ellen coming my way with Shasta on a leash. The puppy was in her element — sniffing everything and delighting in all the attention that she was getting along the way. I think it took Ellen a good ten minutes to walk the line of vendors to our booths.

"Looks like you are accompanied by Miss Personality," I said as Ellen drew near.

"She does seem to enjoy the attention," Ellen answered. ""We'll see how she handles a few hours of it at the booth. My guess is I'll have one tired and worn-out puppy before our shift is done."

"Since it wears out the adults, I'm sure you're right. Denali just had her share of fur-pulling and baby loves. She gave me one of those looks that says, 'You owe me' before I extracted her from it. But when the woman was buying a considerable amount of handspun yarn, moving her along on her way too fast didn't seem wise."

"Seems reasonable to me, but I can understand Nali's point of view."

With that, Ellen moved on to the Pyr booth and I turned to help another customer. I felt more than noticed someone go behind me to the back of the booth, but didn't get a chance to turn around immediately. When I did, I found Dorothy Swanson squatting down talking quietly to Nali.

"Hey lady, good to see you," I said as I walked over and gave her a big hug. "I'm surprised that I haven't before now. You must be busy over in the stables with your critters."

"They do take up time, especially since people have been interested in the lambs that I have for sale. But I've also been trying to take in as much of the fleece judging as possible. I can almost always count on learning something new to help me with my entries for the next year. So far, I've gotten three blues and a red, so I'm pretty happy."

"I guess. Which breeds?"

"Two blues for Romney and a blue and red for Blue Faced Leicester. The Corriedale, including the one I told you about, are still waiting to be judged."

"I'll have to look for the Corriedale. They are a favorite spinning breed for me, and I like the BFL too. Could be an expensive Gathering for me."

"Oh, you'll turn it back into profit if I know you, but that's not really why I'm here. I need to talk to you about Great Pyrenees. Oh, and you too, Ellen," she said as she noticed Ellen in the Pyr booth next door. "I've lost one more lamb and another ewe to predator attacks. I've got to do something about it, and you say that you have a solution."

"We do, Dorothy. It has four feet, a loud bark, lots of hair, and a mouth full of teeth if they are necessary. You've met Denali and this fluff ball is Shasta," I said as Shasta squirreled under the Pyr booth table and ended up on my side.

"Denali is partnered with my male, Falcor, to guard my herd and property. Shasta is learning the ropes to help Tahoma take care of Ellen's."

"I notice that you both have two dogs and one of each sex. Do you breed them?"

"We have two dogs because backup is a good thing if you get hit with a large predator or with dogs," I answered, "and they are of opposite sex because you can get very nasty same sex fights with some of the dogs. We don't breed; it's better to have them altered if you're going to have them guard livestock. It prevents hormones from taking their minds off their jobs. Also if you have a bitch who isn't altered, you will lose her working ability to heats at least twice a year and to pregnancy if she's bred."

"As you know from being a sheep breeder," Ellen chimed in, "there is a lot more to breeding than just having two willing animals of opposite sexes. That goes for breeding dogs too. That's why we leave the breeding of Pyrs to the experts."

"That makes sense," Dorothy said. "and they really do their job?"

"They do their job incredibly well," Ellen answered. "Before I got Tahoma, I was losing a lamb or two every lambing season and you have to remember that I have a small flock and heavily fenced pastures. I have not lost a single one since he arrived on the place. I have just added Shasta and I know she will be a big help to Tahoma."

"I have never had a predation loss," I added. "But I had Nali before I got my first sheep. She was a companion first and then a livestock dog."

"Does that work?" Dorothy asked.

"In my situation it did because I have such a small flock and they are kept pastured close to the house. For you, it would not work. You'll need to train your Pyr to stay with the livestock, but that doesn't bother them. It's what they were bred to do, and they do it happily and well."

"Well, I have to do something and this just may be the answer. Fencing alone sure doesn't do it. And I don't want to poison; it's too indiscriminate. Trapping and shooting aren't very good solutions either."

"Why don't I lend you a book on using livestock guardian dogs? I can bring it with me tomorrow, and you can get the names of some excellent breeders right here in western Washington from the information at the booth where Ellen and Shasta are working. You can call them and talk to them about puppy availability and about using LGDs."

"That sounds great, and I suppose I can still bend the ears of the two of you."

"Absolutely," both Ellen and I said at the same time and then laughed at our penchant for doing that from time to time.

"I can't get over how calm these two are," Dorothy remarked. "My border collies would be all over the place, and they've just lain down next to each other at the back of your booth after greeting me."

"That's one of the pleasures of living with LGDs," I said. "They say hello and then they find themselves a place to lie down. They're not in your face all the time."

"I think I could come to like that," Dorothy responded. "I might have to eventually get me one for a barn and house dog too."

Ellen laughed. "They're addictive. Most people can't have just one."

"Another thing we didn't mention," I said, "is these guys are not allowed outside a fence or off a leash when you're talking suburban farming like all of us are doing. They will stake territory much bigger than your land and go on walkabout on a regular basis. This puts them in jeopardy and doesn't help your problem."

"I don't have a problem with that," Dorothy said. "Given the problem I have with loose dogs and predation, I obviously am not one to think that dogs should be allowed to roam; and I have good fences."

"By the way," I added, " Catalin Ezkarra mentioned on Wednesday that she had eight Pyrenees working protecting her flock. So you can see that she believed in them."

"It really is tragic that she was killed in such a senseless accident," Dorothy said.

"Ellen and I aren't so sure it was an accident," I stated. "The llama seemed to be quite gentle and tame and everyone says that she was a marvel with animals even if she had problems with people."

"She did have a problem with people, that's for sure. I couldn't believe it when she kicked Sheila out. Sheila was her shield from the world. She did all the outside contact stuff and that left Catalin free to work with her animals where she excelled."

"Did you know her, Dorothy?" I asked.

"Have for years. She bought her property from my father when he decided to cut back on our acreage. She was a young gal then, right out of ag school at WSU."

"So does your spread connect with hers?"

"Yep, on one corner. It's one reason my father decided to sell the acreage. Our original spread was a crazy quilt of patched-together pieces that looked like two rectangles gathered together on point. By selling off that area, we both ended up with a rectangular piece of a decent size to run the amount of livestock we wanted to deal with. Rex's land abuts hers along one side on the opposite side from where I am."

"Do you know what the problem was between she and Rex? I mean, beside the minor problems with the stalls here."

"Yeeees. I didn't know that was part of the town gossip, though."

"I don't think it is. But when she and Rex were at each other's throats Wednesday afternoon, she accused him of bringing their personal fight into the assigning of stalls and later I overheard Rex telling someone that the woman was driving him nuts with the dispute."

"Catalin accused Rex of stealing twenty acres of her land that included a section with a lovely creek running through it. None of us know why she started it. The land is his. Sheila pointed that out to her. That's why Catalin threw her out. She accused Sheila of taking his side and plotting against her."

"Could she have convinced the court to give her the property?" I asked.

"Who knows? It's sometimes interesting what people can manage to get through the courts. But as far as I know, she hadn't gotten that far yet. She was still just trying to bully him out of it. And then there was something going on about a prize ram that I never quite understood, but Rex has it and Catalin was also claiming that it was hers."

"So her death solved a lot of problems for him. Especially since whoever inherits the ranch will probably not carry on her pursuits in that area," I commented.

"Yep, but I can't imagine that Rex would kill her for a property dispute."

"Well, to be honest, I can't either; but I've learned recently that sometimes the person you least expect may be capable of murder. And he was sure furious with her Wednesday afternoon. Could he have gotten in another argument with her and then had something happen in a fit of anger?"

"I suppose so, but I really doubt it. That just isn't Rex."

"Just isn't Rex how?" Ellen said as she joined the conversation again after being busy with the Pyr booth.

"I'll tell you later," I said because I had spotted Rex moving down the aisle, stopping to talk to various vendors.

Dorothy noticed him just as I did and nodded. "And I need to get over to the fleece judging and see what pearls of wisdom I can glean."

"Enjoy the judging. If you see a really nice one let me know," I said as she headed for the judging area. I turned back to say something to Ellen just as Rex walked up.

"Hey, Martha, have you seen Mark?"

"Nope. Is he supposed to be here? He usually has office hours at this time."

"There's a lamb in the stable building that may be sick. I wanted him to take a look at it. We can't afford to have anything passed to other animals."

"I agree with you on that," I said. "None of us want to pick up something that could move through our flocks, especially those with large flocks. Where will you be if I see him before you do?"

"I'm going back out into the stable. Send him that way if he comes in here."

"Will do."

I watched Rex as he walked out the door next to the Pyr booth and headed across the area between the two buildings. Could he have been the one to kill Catalin? I hoped not. I really liked the man.

I then turned my attention to customers at my booth and put Rex, and Catalin's death, out of my mind for awhile.

Chapter 10

"Hey, lady, want some lunch?" I looked up from once again organizing my yarn on a table to see Mark standing at the edge of my booth while still managing to pet the Pyr closest to him in the club booth. Denali noticed him at the same time and decided that he could just as well pet her and wandered up to sit next to him.

"Sure, what've you got in mind?"

"The local scout troop has some pretty good burgers in their booth, or Black Hills Cafe has a booth with soup and bread, and I think I heard that the boosters would have chili."

"I had the boosters' chili yesterday and it was good, but I'd love Portuguese bean soup. Think Sally'd have it here?"

"Probably, it's one of her specialties. Shall I check?"

"Yep. I'll take anything except clam chowder, but my preference is the bean." For some reason, in spite of living in all kinds of areas that specialize in clam chowder, it still was my least favorite of soups.

"OK, be back in a jiffy. Want me to take Denali with me?"

"She'd love that. She's been cooped up in here for some time, but it'll take you longer. She's a regular social butterfly."

"That's no problem. We're not in any hurry."

"OK, here's her leash."

I watched as Mark walked off with my dog. He'd saved her life a couple of months ago and they had a special bond. Mark and I were moving in that direction too, although I was still a little wary of that development. Not that I didn't like Mark. I did and I admired him a great deal, but John had been the love of my life and moving into anything other than friendship with another man was a giant leap for me. However, Mark was pretty special. We'd just have to see how things went. Like Mark and Nali, I was in no hurry. I went back to organizing the yarn that Mark's visit had interrupted. Some Gathering visitors browsed by picking up and moving yarn all around as they were making up their minds, and I seemed to have had my share of those this morning.

"Would this yarn work for a hat?"

I turned to see a petite teenager with sparkling hazel eyes and long blond hair holding a skein of my handspun.

"Probably. What kind of hat did you have in mind?"

"Just something simple, maybe a watch cap. I'm a beginning knitter, but I want to make a hat for my boyfriend. He loves to hike and climb in the mountains, and it can get cold up there."

"It can," I said. "This will be perfect for that. It's mainly wool, which is warm even when it is wet, and it has the added warmth of a small amount of dog hair in it."

"Like from those dogs?" she asked, pointing at the Pyrs in the booth next door.

"Yes," I answered. "Actually from that dog," I added, point-ing at Nali as she wandered toward the booth with Mark at her side.

"Oh, she's beautiful. Will you take my picture with her?" she asked, handing me her cell phone. Then I can put it with the hat when I give it to him.

"Well, let's ask her if she thinks it's a good idea." I turned to Nali. "Want to have your picture taken, big girl?"

Nali answered by going to check out the young woman, who immediately crouched down to be at Nali's level. Nali must have decided that she was OK because she gave her a snuffle and then put her head on the young woman's knee. The girl looked up at me and grinned as I snapped the picture.

"Here, hold your yarn," I said as I handed her the skein.

"Like this," she said as she let it drape over Nali's shoulder.

"That will do." I chuckled a bit as I snapped a second pic-ture.

Getting up from talking to Nali, she handed me the skein and added, "My name is Andrea."

"Hello, Andrea. I'm Martha and your new friend is Denali. Do you need a pattern to go with your yarn?"

"No, I have one in a magazine, but can I call you if I need some help?"

"Sure thing. I'll put a business card in with your yarn. You can call or come by the shop. We're normally open Tuesday through Saturday. Events like this can change that, though, so if it's a distance for you to drive, you might want to call before you come."

"I'll do that," Andrea said as she paid me for the yarn. "Bye, Denali, maybe I'll see you again."

Nali answered with a slow wag of her tail.

"Ready for lunch?" Mark asked. "Got us some of Sally's crusty bread to go with it, and she did have Portuguese bean soup."

"Good, I'm starving. Ellen, can you keep an eye on my booth for half an hour or so? I'll bring you back some soup of your own." She answered with a grin and a nod of her head as she listened to a question from a woman at the Pyr booth.

Mark, Denali and I made our way out of the arena building and over to a solitary picnic table located in the shade between a couple of the buildings.

"I'm assuming you found Rex and have seen to the possible sick lamb," I said as we settled onto the benches and opened our soup containers. Nali settled herself under the table in the shade.

"Yep, I don't think it's anything serious. He seemed a little lethargic, but there was no fever and no real signs of illness. It's probably the stress of the show. I suggested that he be taken home both to protect other animals just in case and for his sake too. They were making arrangements to do that when I left."

"Good, these events can be very stressful for the animals. It is one reason that I try to give mine some break time whenever I can."

"Good idea. Denali looks pretty stressed out at the moment," Mark said with a grin as he looked at my big girl curled up sound asleep by our feet.

"She and Falcor handle it very well, but even they sleep like the dead when I bring them home from one of these. They'll tell you that guarding their flock all day is a much easier job than supervising humans."

"I'll bet. I find supervising humans stressful too."

I chuckled as I spooned up another mouthful of the

wonderful soup and sighed. "Sally makes the best bean soup on this side of the state, I swear."

"She does and the bread is just the thing to go with it. I'm glad that she decided to have a booth this year. Other people must have been too because there was quite a line. On another note," Mark continued, "I overheard some interesting gossip while I was in the stable."

"What? Tell me; don't tease,"

"Well, evidently Rex and Catalin had a major argument again on Wednesday evening just before it got dark. One of the women who's sleeping in the stable with her animals overheard them. She wasn't close enough to hear what they were arguing about, but she said they were toe to toe, going at it hammer and tong."

"I guess they had a lot of bad blood between them. Raises all kinds of questions about her death, doesn't it? I like Rex. I sure don't want him to be a murderer, but we both know of someone who fit that category before. I've learned that even the best people can sometimes do horrible things."

"I know. It could have still been an accident in the llama's stall. But he's so calm and easy at my place in quarantine that I have my doubts. Just don't you do anything foolish. I don't like patching up animals I care a lot about and I sure don't want to find out that you need to be patched up or worse."

"I won't, I promise. Well, I need to pick up Ellen's soup and get back to my booth or she's going to be wanting commissions for all her work."

"I have a full appointment schedule too. Do you want to have dinner someplace on Sunday after all this is done?"

"Sounds good, but let me get back to you on it. Sometimes all I want to do is crash at the end of these things."

"OK. I'll take care of this stuff," he said as he gathered up our trash. "See you soon."

I watched as he walked off toward the parking lot with his long graceful stride. He was one of the most handsome and genuine men I'd ever met. He walked in beauty in every way. I turned and Nali and I walked over to the Black Hills Cafe booth. Soon we had Ellen's soup and were walking through the door into the arena. There was a crowd around the Pyr booth and Ellen was talking at my booth to a small, older woman with short gray hair wearing a peasant skirt. Looked like I did need to get back to work.

"Oh, here comes Martha," Ellen said. "She can help you much better than I can.

"Thanks, Ellen," I said as I handed her the bag holding her soup and bread. "Your turn for a break."

"Hi, what can I do for you?" I asked, giving my attention to my customer.

She turned to face me directly. Her face was wrinkled in a way that said that she smiled often and indeed, she was smiling now with both her deep brown eyes and her mouth. "I'd like to take up spinning, but I haven't a clue what I need to start. Can you point me in the right direction?" she asked.

"I think so. Do you want to start with a spindle or a wheel?"

"I don't know. Is one easier than the other?"

"Not really, I explained. They are slightly different in what you do with your hands, and your feet aren't involved with a spindle, but the principles are the same. There is a large differ-ence in your beginning investment, though, so I often suggest starting with a spindle if you aren't totally sure this is something you want to do."

"What would I need to start if I used a spindle?"

"Two things," I said, "a spindle and some fiber to spin. I'd recommend a wool that has a medium-length staple. A lot of people like Romney because it's a beginner-friendly breed. It is not as soft as some breeds, but it's very easy to spin. Here, let me show you some different examples of possible fiber for you."

I began to pull out different types of roving and top for her. "This," I said as I showed her a beautiful teal-colored roving, "is a cross between a Romney and a Corriedale and comes from a local breeder who is also a spinner. While this beautiful, natural-colored roving," I added, as I showed her some lovely gray fiber, "comes from a purebred Corriedale. It too is from a local breeder. It's a fleece that I purchased and then sent to a local processor to turn it into roving."

"They are both beautiful," she said.

"Before you make up your mind," I added, "let me show you some examples of commercial top." I pulled out some beautiful top from a different spot in my booth. "This red blend and the green one are both merino, which is a breed with one of the softest fleece and a usually a shorter staple length."

"They are all lovely, but now I'm confused," she said. "What's the difference between roving and top?"

"That's a good question and you can get different answers depending on whom you ask. Although technically roving will always have some twist added to it during its preparation and can be either carded or combed, that isn't the way most people use the term. Usually when people talk of roving, they mean that the fiber has been carded and the fibers will be in multiple directions. Top, on the other hand, has been combed, which removes shorter fibers and small pieces of fiber called noils and puts the fiber in parallel lines. Which you choose depends to some extent on how you want to spin it."

"I think I like the natural-colored roving. Would that work well for me?"

"I'd say it's an excellent choice. Now let's find a spindle for you."

I led her over to the basket where I had spindles and pulled out three that I thought would be good for a beginner. All were around one and a half ounces.

"Since you really have done no spinning, you aren't going to be able to tell which one will spin best for you. However, I can guarantee you that they are all excellent spinners, and I've tested all of them. So why don't you see which one just feels best in your hands and which one you like the best?"

She picked each one up and hefted it in her right hand. Then she ran her hands over them and rubbed them against her cheek. She was obviously a person who liked the tactile feeling of good wood.

"I think I like this one best," she said, after looking them all over a second time.

"That is made by a woodturner in Hawai`i," I said. "The wood is spalted mango. Spalted just means that the wood was allowed to be attacked by fungus for a period of time. It is what gives it the lovely dark markings."

"OK, I have my supplies picked out, but how do I use them?"

"Hopefully we can solve that; these come with three private lessons at my shop. Are you local?"

"I live in Elma so I can come to Black Hills easily," she said.

"That's good, however, I won't be in the shop until next Tuesday; so if you are in a hurry, I'd suggest that you use the internet and look at some of the great YouTube videos out there. There are also some excellent books and DVDs available, but I think you'd have a better idea of what you want after you have done a little spinning with me."

"That sounds good; I'll be there Tuesday afternoon. My name is Deirdre Watanabe. My husband is from a Japanese family in Hawai`i," she added as I looked up from packing her things when I heard the last name.

I smiled. "I'm Martha Williamson; I've put a business card in with your purchases in case you need to contact me. My shop is easy to find. It's right on the road going into Black Hills. I lived in Hawai`i for a few years with my husband and was actually born there, although I remember none of that time. We left when I was very young. My father was an Air Force officer."

"Oh, good, that'll give us something else in common to talk about," she said. "I love Hawai`i. Well, I've taken a ton of your time, Martha. Thank you for all of your help."

"It was my pleasure. That's why the booth is here. See you soon."

I watched as she wandered up the line of booths, fingering some of the lovely fiber, and stopped two booths up to ask a question. Then I turned to put away the items that I had pulled out to show her.

"That took you quite awhile," Ellen said from the Pyr booth.

"It did, but I think I may well have a new convert and maybe a friend. That's always fun."

After a busy hour with little time to breathe, I got a lull and noticed that the Pyr booth had also slowed down. Plus there were three people in addition to Ellen there right now.

"Would you mind keeping an eye on things for me again? I think Denali could use a break outside and I'd like to check on Juan and Joseph."

"No problem. I'll just keep them talking until you come back if I can't answer their questions. That's what I did with the last one. What did she say her name was?"

"Deirdre Watanabe. She lives in Elma and has Hawai`i connections so it will be fun to get to know her better."

"Well, take off. Part of my extra help leaves in about an hour."

"Denali, we have our marching orders. Let's go before she changes her mind," I said as I reached for Nali's leash.

I took Denali out the door next to the Pyr booth and gave her some time on a patch of grass to sniff and do her business. Then because the day was so pleasant, I decided to walk around the building on the outside to the door, which would give me access to the horse stalls and Juan and Joseph.

Back inside and with my eyes adjusted again to the dimness of the building, I caught a glimpse of movement that seemed to be in the stall where Catalin was murdered. Denali and I walked down the aisle between the stalls and the wall that separated the stall area from the arena floor. As I got closer to the stall, I was sure there was someone in it, but I couldn't quite make out who. However, Denali gave a low rumble deep in her throat. This area was fairly deserted at the moment and I guess she wasn't totally happy with what she sensed. As we approached the stall, she moved between me and the entrance to it. It was at that point that I realized it was Kelmen, Catalin's nephew, who was in the stall. His back was to me and he hadn't noticed Denali and me yet.

"That stall is off limits to people attending the Gathering," I said. "That's why the tape was there which I see you've ignored."

He jumped at the sound of my voice and whirled around.

"Huh, I was just trying to see where she died. I mean, I still can't believe that she's dead, and thought if I looked it might make it seem more real to me."

"You could have done that from outside the tape. I suggest

you leave now or I will call Sheriff Green."

"OK," he said, but his face spoke volumes about his feelings of getting kicked out. "I'm leaving, but I sure wish someone would explain to me how a gentle llama could kill my aunt. She was a wizard with animals."

"I don't know, Kelmen," I admitted. "Maybe she just stumbled and fell, hitting her head." I had no intention of sharing my feelings that she had been murdered with Kelmen. "By the way, didn't I see you at the Indian casino last night?"

He gave me a quizzical look. "You must be mistaken. I was home studying for a test."

"I guess I must have been," I said. "It must have been someone who looked like you in passing."

"I'm sure it was. OK, I'm out of here. I think I'll go and see if I can find Sheila. At least we both loved my aunt. I feel like no one here even cares that she died. Look at them all busy making sales and acting as if nothing happened."

With that, he turned and headed off down the aisle. I watched him go, wondering if I really had seen him last night, and if it was him, why had he decided to lie to me? Just what was he hiding?

Well, I needed to check on my animals and get back to my booth. Nali and I proceeded down the aisle to the stall where Juan and Joseph were housed. I opened the stall and Nali preceded me into the area. She moved up and sniffed the alpaca to make sure that all was well. I checked their food and water to make sure they had plenty of both. Then, giving each of them a small carrot, I turned to leave the stall. Nali stood there for a minute as if deciding whether to stay there or come with me. Then with a wag of her tail, she again preceded me through the door.

"OK, big girl, we need to get back to our booth. Ellen is going to think that we've deserted her completely." Nali just looked at me and headed down the aisle toward the door that would lead us back into the arena area.

"I'd about decided that you were gone forever," Ellen said as Nali and I came into sight. "Luckily, the questions have been simple and I was able to make a few sales without having any meltdowns."

"Glad to hear it. Although I can't imagine you melting down even with the most difficult of questions. You're very good at punting."

"Ah, discovered," she said with a grin.

I got Nali settled back in the rear of the booth and checked over the sales that Ellen had made. Everything was in order; as always, my best friend had come through for me.

Noticing that Ellen was not busy at the Pyr booth, I signaled for her to come over to mine. "Guess who I found messing around in the stall where Catalin was killed."

"Haven't a clue. Tell me."

"Kelmen. He claimed that he was trying to make her death real to him, but I think he was looking for something and I interrupted that hunt. He also denied being at the casino last night. Said that he was home studying for a test."

"That's interesting," Ellen said, "since you were pretty certain that the young man you saw was he."

"If you are talking about Kelmen Ezkarra, he should be home studying for a test." This came from a short, rather heavyset young woman with spiky black hair and multiple earrings in her ears at the booth next to us.

"I'm sorry, but I couldn't help overhearing you. I'm Marcia Phillips and I'm helping my mother in her booth for the afternoon."

"Hi, Marcia, I'm Martha Williamson and this is Ellen Goodson; I've known your mother for a number of years and love her beautiful hand wovenrugs. It's good to meet you, but what were you saying about Kelmen?"

"Just that he should be home studying. I'm in two classes with him at the community college and he's close to flunking out of both of them. His grades aren't good and his attendance is worse. I don't know how he expects to finish his AA degree this year given his attention to his classes right now."

"That's interesting," I said. "When I talked to him yesterday, he sounded like he was quite involved in his studies and talked of joining his aunt on her ranch when he graduated."

"He was up until a few months ago, but something happened around November and his whole attitude changed. He got through winter quarter by the skin of his teeth and I'm not sure he'll make it at all this quarter."

"Do you have any idea what might have caused the change?"

"I don't. He and I weren't close before although we did talk about the classes we had in common and a couple of times we studied together for a test. But as his performance began to slide, he became more and more distant. I've no idea what's going on. I wondered if he'd had a falling out with his aunt. He relied on her for his college expenses."

Just as she finished her sentence, a woman walked up to her mother's booth. She waved to us and went over to help her.

"That's interesting," I said to Ellen. "I wonder what's going on there."

"I don't know, but I see a whole passel of children coming toward us and I know what a child magnet these dogs are. I think I'm going to be busy for awhile."

With that she turned her attention to the children and the

big white dogs. It was a matter of protecting both from the other, but mainly protecting the dogs.

Chapter 11

Since things were slow for me at the moment, I pulled out my spinning wheel and started working on some Blue Faced Leicester roving. It was a piece of wool that I could allow to become a sample if someone came along who wanted to try spinning with the wheel. If that didn't happen, I'd have some yarn for whatever purpose I wanted to use it. I was just getting started with it when I noticed Elizabeth Swanson. Her short, slightly plump figure and sleek, short dark brown hair became visible as she wandered out of a booth and back into the next one without taking a whole lot of time in any of them. I continued spinning as she came up to my booth.

"You know, I really should get one of those things," she said as she eyed the wheel. "I'm enjoying the spindle, but I think I'd like to do things a little faster."

Elizabeth had taken my spinning class in February and had taken to it like the fiber fan that she was.

"Some people say a spindle gives you more yarn," I commented, "but my guess is that for you it probably doesn't. You're like me and if you need a portable project, you take your knitting. The people who get more yardage out of a spindle, take their spindles with them everywhere so that it comes out at every stop where they have to wait for some reason. You do that with your knitting."

"That's right. I do most of my spinning when Dave and I are watching television or a movie in the evenings or just sitting around listening to music in front of the fire. It seems to me that I could get more done if I had a wheel there in reach of my chair." Elizabeth was married to my friend and lawyer, David Swanson. Actually, he was the lawyer for most of the town and outlying areas.

"You could," I said, "and I'd love to sell you one. Check this one out, but don't make up your mind yet. You need to come by the store so you can check out the different styles and models that I have there. Here take my chair and I'll get you started."

She sat down where I was sitting and I broke off the roving that I was working on. I was going to have her just work with her feet for a bit, and it would pull any roving still in front of the orifice onto the bobbin.

"This is a double treadle wheel, which means that you use both of your feet to run it, alternating one foot and then the other."

"Like this," she said and then started to laugh as she mixed her feet up a bit. But she was soon working them smoothly and correctly.

"OK, now we will add the hands. Let me sit there a moment and get the roving started again for you. This is the way the yarn feeds," I said as I moved into the chair and fished it back off the bobbin and ran it through the guide hooks and out through the orifice. "You join fiber with a spinning wheel the same way as you do with a spindle, and the drafting is done much the same way. When you get a length of yarn, you lessen your tension on the spun yarn and let the bobbin take up the yarn." I demonstrated for a short while. "OK, now you try it."

She took my place at the wheel and got her hands in position on the fiber.

"Now treadle slowly. This isn't a speed challenge at this point and you will need to learn to draft at the speed that you treadle."

"Oh my," she commented, "this is quite different, but I like it. Oops. What do I do when I get one of those lumps?"

"Those are called slubs," I said. "If you like the look you can leave them in for a designer-type yarn. However, I usually work them out if I get one. Stop treadling. Using your two hands on either side of the slub area, twist in the opposite direction from the one you were spinning so that you open up the fiber. Now draft that slub out to the thickness that you want it and continue spinning to put the twist back into your yarn."

She worked on her yarn as I talked her through it and soon had the slub worked out of her yarn and was continuing on with her spinning.

"I really do like this. I'm going to get one, but you think I should wait and not get it now."

"Yes, I do. This wheel is an Ashford Joy, which is very portable, but it might not be the best choice for you. I have a couple of other models of Ashford wheels at the shop. They are a New Zealand company and make a good solid wheel. But I also have some Lendrum wheels and some Schacht wheels, and I'd like you to try all of them. Lendrum is a Canadian company and Schacht is made in Colorado."

"Ok, I'll come by next week. Probably Tuesday because now that I've played with it, I know I can't live without one."

"Sounds good to me," I said and added with a chuckle, "I love selling things. Other than making me happy by deciding to buy a wheel, what brings you here today."

"I'm doing a reconnoiter to see how I'm going to spend my money tomorrow. I can't really shop until I see how much money I spend on fleece. You did create a monster, you know."

"Plan on getting here early if you want to buy fleece. The best buys will go fast."

"OK, will do. By the way, have you heard anything more on Catalin Ezkarra's death?"

"Nope, as far as I know Jonathon is still treating it as an accident, but neither Ellen nor I like it. We watched her with animals here. She could charm an animal in a second and she moved well around them. I just can't figure her for getting killed because she moved wrong while in a llama stall. It just doesn't figure."

"Bet her family's going to be pissed. Her will leaves everything to her lesbian partner. Everything, that is, except the proceeds from a pretty hefty life insurance policy. That goes to the nephew. The brother gets zip."

"When was the will written?"

"About three years ago and it hasn't been changed since she threw Sheila out of the house."

"I wonder if she was planning on changing it?"

"She hadn't contacted David if she was. But I suppose someone could be worried about that possibility and decide to make sure it didn't happen."

"Someone could, that's true. Or someone might just assume that they would be the beneficiary of the will and not know the real content. Someone like a brother or a nephew."

"Possibly, but it would sure be crazy to take that chance. Murder is pretty dangerous if one gets caught in the long run."

"It is," I said, "but how many murderers think they'll get caught?"

"True. Well, I need to check out the rest of the vendors and then head home for the evening. I'll see you early tomorrow and then again on Tuesday to get my wheel."

"Sounds like a plan. Have a great evening and tell David hi for me."

I watched as she crossed over and started down the line of vendors on the other side of the walkway.

The rest of the afternoon went by quickly with people coming and going. I made quite a few good sales and set up some private lessons for next week when I would be back in the shop. It is important that buyers have a good experience with their new equipment from the beginning, and I've found that a short private lesson almost always guarantees that will happen.

"If you want to take any kind of a break before the evening onslaught, you need to do it now," Ellen said. "I'm done at the Pyr booth. I'll be heading home shortly, but I'm willing to work your booth for awhile so you can take a breather."

"Thanks, I'd like that, and I know Denali would like a walk. Wouldn't you, big girl?" She got to her feet and, with her tail wagging, came over to Ellen and me. "I think I'll wander down and talk to Sheila before we go out. Elizabeth just told me that she will inherit the ranch. I wonder if she knew that."

"Interesting. I'll be anxious to know what you find out.

Well, off with you both. The sooner you get back, the sooner I can go home and put my feet up."

"Come on, Nali," I said as I clipped her leash on. "Let's go see what we can find out."

Nali and I started down the line of vendors with her a little in the lead. However, the progress was slow because of the big, white people magnet and she was delighting in soaking up all the praise about her size, beauty and gentleness. We eventually found Sheila's booth, but Sheila was nowhere to be seen.

"Have you seen Sheila?" I asked the woman in the next booth.

"I heard her ask Aloha on the other side to watch her booth for a bit. That was about half an hour ago and I haven't seen her since."

I moved down to Aloha's booth and noticed that she was selling beautiful quilt items made in the Hawaiian style with needle-turned appliqué and echo quilting.

"Hi, do you know where I could find Sheila?" I asked.

She turned from working with an item at the back of her booth when she heard me and smiled. What a beautiful woman. She had long dark hair, twinkling brown eyes and was obviously of mixed race like so many are from the Islands.

"She took her dog out for a short walk. I expect her back any minute as she usually doesn't stay away this long."

"Thanks, Nali and I are heading out to give her a walk, so maybe I'll find Sheila out on the grounds. Are you from Hawai`i? I'm guessing so with your lovely work, but guesses can be wrong."

"Yes, I was raised outside of Lahaina, but came here to go to Evergreen, fell in love, and stayed."

"I was born in Honolulu while my father was stationed

there and lived on Oahu when my husband was stationed there. It is beautiful and the people are lovely and gracious."

"I miss it some days especially when we get a siege of gray days all strung together, but Washington has become home, and I imagine we'll stay here. Are you a vendor?" she asked as she noticed Nali by my legs.

"Yes, I own The Spider's Web, a fiber shop that centers around making and using yarn."

"Oh yes, I noticed it when I took a quick survey of the different booths. Yours is the one with the handspun yarn, right?"

"That's mine."

"I plan on stopping by before the show's over. The handspun yarn is great for my crazy quilts and art quilts. Since this is my first time at this show, I decided to just bring the Hawaiian work because it's different. I had no idea what kind of competition there would be with the other styles, but it looks like I could have brought all of them."

"Yes, you could have; I think you're the only quilt booth. Do come by and take a look. Or better yet, come by the shop one day and we could have more time to talk and get to know each other."

"That sounds like a wonderful idea. I'll do that."

"Great, I'm open Tuesday through Saturday most of the time. If you have to drive far, give me a call first just to make sure." I reached into my pocket as I said this and pulled out a card and handed it to her. "Well, Nali, you've been patient. It's time for your walk and we'll see if we can find Sheila at the same time. It was great meeting you, Aloha."

Nali and I then turned and continued to walk down the row of vendors to the main doors of the arena and on out into the bright sunshine. Sheila was nowhere to be seen so we headed for a grassy area behind the stables. I let loose of the brake on the flexi-lead and let her wander as she pleased while I took the time to enjoy the late afternoon sun. I wondered a bit as to where Sheila had gone. It isn't like a vendor to leave their booth too long, especially if you're just relying on the vendor in the next booth to cover for you. And speaking of, it was time for me to get back to mine. Even when the person watching your booth is your best friend, it's not cool to make them do it forever. I looked over to where Nali was giving a pile of rocks a good going over with her nose.

"Come on, big girl, it's time for us to go back to the booth." Nali just looked up at me and continued to sort through the rocks with her nose. "Come, Nali," I said as I walked over, shortening the leash as I got closer. Again she looked up, and again her nose went back down to the rocks. Or rock because when I got closer, I realized that she was concentrating on just one rock. "What you got, girl?" I looked closer and noticed that the rock, which was a little larger than the rest in the pile, had rather sharp edges and a brown stain on it.

Again, Nali's nose went to that brown stain and then she looked up at me with questions in her eyes. It didn't smell like a rock and she knew it. I looked at it myself and my mind flashed back to Catalin's head. Was it possible that this was the weapon that would take her death from a questionable accident to murder? Only a lab could tell us that. I reached into my pocket and pulled out my cell phone.

"Black Hills Police," Tammie answered. The lubricant that kept Black Hills Police functioning, she was the daytime dispatcher, answered people's questions, kept tabs on Jonathon, and generally kept everyone up to date and operating smoothly.

"Hi, Tammie, this is Martha Williamson. Is Jonathon around?"

"Sure, Martha, I'll put you through."

"Hey, Martha, what's up?"

"Maybe nothing, Jonathon, but Nali has found something out on the academy grounds that I think you should see and see it where she found it. Want to drive out?"

"You think it's important? I have a ton of paperwork to do and I was just getting a good start on it."

"Yes, I do. I don't want to affect your opinion with mine but I really think you should come check it out."

"OK, it's a lovely afternoon and I hate paperwork so guess I'll be out there. You at your booth?"

"No, I'm sitting on a pile of rocks in the grassy area behind the stables. Nali and I will stay here."

"OK, see you soon."

"Nali, think we should tell Ellen that we'll be out here for a bit?" She just lay down with her head on her paws in a pose that said she thought we were going to be here longer than she wanted to be. "Sorry, big girl, but it's your fault, you know."

I dialed Ellen's cell phone.

"You're calling me rather than rescuing me?" Ellen's voice came over my phone.

"Yep, I'm sitting on a pile of rocks behind the stable. Will fill you in when I get back inside. Can your feet stand a little longer on the hard floor?"

"Probably, but you'll owe me."

"OK, I promise a big payback soon."

"Mark is here. I'll send him out."

"Thanks, I'll see you soon. I'm waiting for Jonathon."

"Now what kind of trouble did you and that white dog get into?"

"Tell you soon, but it's all her fault."

"Sure, blame it on the dog. Well, you have a customer so I'll send Mark out and get busy doing your job."

I smiled as I hung up. I didn't know what I'd do without Ellen. She kept me sane right after John was killed, and she still added delight to my days with her friendship. I figured I might as well enjoy the unexpected ability to sit and enjoy the lovely spring sunshine, so I settled down on the grass next to the rock pile to wait and let my mind wander off to Catalin. What had that woman done to make someone so angry with her?

"Couldn't you have found a more comfortable place to sit in the sun?" I started at the sound of Mark's voice. Nali jumped up and went puppy wiggles all over.

"Better watch that dog," I said and laughed. "I've heard it said that she's vicious."

"Been talking to the coyotes, have you?"

"I wish. Wouldn't it be fascinating to know what they're saying to each other when we hear them in the night?"

"It would, but given a choice, I'd rather understand just plain old dog and cat so I could treat my patients better."

"You have a point there. Ever thought of hiring an animal communicator?"

"Nope, but I find the concept interesting. Would look into it more for myself if I only had time to breathe."

"Speaking of, aren't you done a little early for a Friday afternoon?"

"I blocked off the last two appointments of the afternoon so that I could come out here and check on things and then my last appointment went faster than expected. Gave me a breather to see you before Rex and I do a walkthrough among all the animals to make sure everyone looks healthy and well cared for while they're here.

"And speaking of, here he comes along with Jonathon. So I'll let you get on to your task and I'll talk to Jonathon. Come by the booth before you take off for the evening."

"Will do."

Mark got up and met Rex and Jonathon before they got to me, then moved off with Rex for the stables. I was so glad that he was a man quick on the small signals. He realized that I didn't want Rex to be part of my conversation with Jonathon even though I hadn't verbalized it.

"OK, so how come was I rescued from paperwork?" Jonathon said as he walked up to Nali and me. "And hi, Nali, what have you been up to today that has your mother so keen on seeing me?"

"Nali, let's show Jonathon what you found." I was starting to point it out when Nali moved over and put her nose on the rock that she had singled out earlier. Damn, I think that girl totally understands English, even if my dog is less than optimal. "That's it, Jonathon," I said.

He stooped down and looked at it in the place that it lay.

"Did you touch it or move it?"

"I didn't and I don't think Nali moved it either. She was just going over the rocks with her nose, not pawing at any of them."

"That stain does look ominous," Jonathon said, "and the rock doesn't look like the rest of the pile. It's like someone tossed it here in hopes that it wouldn't be noticed among the rest."

"I doubt that any of the people wandering around the grounds would have picked it out. The dogs are different. I think any of them that came this way would have picked it out of the pile."

"I'm glad it was you and Nali then," Jonathon said this as he reached into his pocket for an evidence bag and picked up the rock. "I'll take it in and get it tested, but this may well mean that you and the other champions of the llama were correct. Can't say that I'm surprised. I was quietly working some of the angles because like you, I didn't really think the evidence added up to an accident. It's nice, though, when the perpetrator thinks he's gotten away with it."

"I've got another couple of hours here tonight," I said. "But do you want to come by the house after I get home to hear the gossip I've picked up the last few days? I've some leftover chili that could make a late supper for us."

"Might be a good idea at that. OK, I'll be there around eight o'clock."

Jonathon headed toward the parking lot and Nali and I moved in the direction of the side door to the arena and my booth inside.

"It's been a crazy afternoon, big girl. I'm sure glad that Ellen was here to help out, aren't you?"

The last was said as we drew close to the booth.

"You better be glad that Ellen was here. Now tell me what kept me here for so much longer than expected this afternoon."

I quickly filled her in on what Nali had found and the fact that Jonathon was coming over this evening to compare notes.

"Want me to come over too?"

"To chaperone or add help with the mystery detection?"

"Maybe a bit of both," she said with a twinkle in her eye.

"I don't think so," I said. "A chaperone isn't needed and we have pretty much shared our ideas so I can convey all the information we have."

"OK, if you say so. Actually what my body really wants is a long hot soak in the bath followed by putting my feet up. So I won't argue with you."

"Argue with you about what?" Mark asked as he walked up.

"Jonathon is coming over to compare notes on Catalin's death this evening, and I told Ellen that I really didn't need her to come over too."

"How about me, should I be there?"

I smiled. Was I seeing just a bit of jealousy here?

"No. As I told Ellen, I don't need a chaperone and I think you and I have pretty well compared notes so that I convey your ideas to Jonathon too."

"Are you sure?"

"I'm sure. I have to be here early tomorrow so I don't antici-pate it to last long and once I've sent Jonathon on his way, I'll be very quickly to bed. Did you and Rex find anything out of the ordinary in your walkthrough?"

"No. We made sure that Catalin's sheep were taken care of since it didn't look like Sheila'd been there since sometime this morning. That seems a little odd, but I guess she could have gotten busy with her booth."

"It doesn't seem like her, I agree. Glad you and Rex handled it. I'm still thinking about one of her Jacob ewes to add to my flock. She has really nice sheep."

"She does. They're well bred and healthy. You could do a lot worse."

"Well, I'll think about it. None of them will be available for awhile. I'm sure there will be questions on who really owns them no matter what the will says."

"I have a feeling that you are correct there. I can't imagine her brother letting the ranch go to Sheila without a fight. Well, Ellen," Mark added, turning to her, "since she doesn't want our company tonight, want to walk out to the parking lot with me?"

"Will do, Mark. You take care, lady, and if Jonathon tells

you anything interesting, be sure and let me know. You know I'm always up until late."

"I'm sure whatever I learn can wait until tomorrow, but if I learn anything startling, I'll let you know."

She gathered up Shasta, and I watched them walk down the line of vendors together. Then Nali and I got busy arranging the booth so that it would be ready for customers in the morning. Saturday was always the busiest day of the show because the fleece went on sale first thing in the morning. There were always plenty of fleeces, but the blue ribbon winners went fast. I would be there myself looking for the Corriedale that Dorothy mentioned Wednesday afternoon. Just as I thought of her, I looked up to see Dorothy coming down the row of vendors.

"How are things going?" I asked her.

"Good, I've sold three of the lambs that I brought. I just have two more and it'll be a clean sweep in that area. Hopefully the fleece sale will go as well tomorrow too."

"I'll be looking for that Corriedale that you told me about."

"Great. It did take a blue. I thought it might. By the way, while I was watching the judging the last two days, I spotted a beautiful natural-colored mohair in a very light silver color and a beautiful brown Shetland that is so dark it's almost black. You might want to watch for them too. The mohair is nice enough, it could end up in the silent auction."

The silent auction is where they sell the top winning fleece of all varieties.

"Thanks for the tip. I'll have to check them out. Although if the mohair does end up in the auction, I may have to let it pass. It's too hard to keep track of bids when you are trying to run a booth."

"You could always put your top bid in as your only bid and

see what that does for you. Of course, it means you miss out on maybe getting it for less."

"I could do that. But if I'm lucky, it won't end up in the auction. I could use some nice mohair for blends."

"I need to check on livestock one more time and then it's home for me so I'll be running. Just wanted to let you know about the fleece."

"Thanks, I appreciate it. Enjoy your evening and I'll see you tomorrow. Don't forget I'm bringing that book in for you."

"I won't." She waved as she walked out the side door.

The last two hours of the show went by quickly and I made a surprising number of sales. But soon it was time to shut things down, check on Juan and Joseph, and take Nali and me home for the evening. I would get there with just enough time to freshen up and heat the chili before Jonathon arrived.

Chapter 12

Falcor welcomed us home as we drove onto the property.
I parked the van and, after putting Nali on her leash, we
went through the inner gate and joined him. He gave
Nali a once-over to make sure she was OK and he knew where
she'd been all day. Then they took off across the field to check
things out together and to let Nali stretch her legs.

I went on into the barn, and made sure that my sheep and
goat had fresh food and water and were in for the evening. This
year's lambs were all doing well and came up for some special
attention before turning back to their dinner. Lei and Ginger
were going to Ellen soon. I was keeping Maile in addition to
the lamb wether, Koma.

With the animals taken care of, I returned to the house. I
could just manage a quick shower before Jonathon arrived. I put
the chili on the stove on low to start heating and headed for the
bathroom. It took me very little time to get clean and changed

into some fresh jeans and a light sweater. Feeling much better, I got back into the kitchen just in time to stir the chili before I heard my dog alarm go off and saw Jonathon's truck pull into my driveway. I opened the back door and stepped out onto the large porch that surrounded the house, giving me a lot of pleasant outside living area during whatever warm weather we managed to have each year.

"Hey," Jonathon said as he bounded up the steps. "I stopped by the bakery and got us some good French bread to go with that chili."

"Sounds great, and I have some salad too so we should be in great shape."

Knowing my habit from living in Hawai`i for so many years, Jonathon kicked off his boots as he entered the house.

"Chili's just about ready," I said. "Are you off duty? Do you want a beer to go with the chili?"

"I am and I do. Want me to get it?"

"Yep, you have a choice from a couple of different microbreweries. Bring me whatever you decide to get for yourself."

"Haven't had anything from Kona before so think I'll try that."

"Fine with me. That's a holdover like the no shoes from the years John and I were in Hawai`i. It was one of his favorites and pretty high on my list too."

Jonathon got the beer out and by searching a couple of cupboards found my beer glasses. He poured our beer and put it on the table while I got the salad, bread and bowls of chili in place. Soon we were seated and ready to eat.

"OK, ma'am, how about you catch me up on what you and Ellen have been up to the last couple of days, since I'm sure that you didn't buy the accidental death for a minute."

"Well, you could hardly expect us to. Catalin was known for her ability to handle animals. Everyone commented on it, whether they liked her or not. Why in the world would she get herself in a position with a large llama where he could harm her? It just didn't make sense. And it wasn't her animal, so why would she even be in there. Ranchers just don't enter stalls with other people's livestock in them. The only exception might be if the animal was in distress and needed immediate attention. That sure wasn't the case with that healthy boy."

"I agree."

"So why did you even let the preliminary assessment of the coroner's office go unchallenged?"

"It let the Gathering keep going, for one thing, which meant that all the people who planned on being there would stick around. They were a good source of information and it was quite possible that one of them killed her. And as I said this afternoon, it let the perpetrator think that he might have gotten away with it."

"OK, so who do you think did it?"

"I have a couple of possibilities, but nothing that could tie anyone up with a bow. Why don't you give me your potentials and we'll see how close we are to matching."

So I ran down our list of Rex, Sheila, Kelmen and Joseba and what we had learned about each one of them.

"That's pretty much the same list I have, and I hadn't heard about the additional fight between Rex and Catalin on Wednesday evening. Nothing we have is strong on any of them. All of it's mainly hearsay and conjecture, and at the moment, we don't even have a solid murder on our hands. Although, the rock you found may change that. If it turns out to have Catalin's blood on it, and I think it does, we then have a probable murder weapon, and I can open an official investigation."

"So I gather then that you just want us to keep our eyes and ears open and keep you up to date on anything we hear."

"That's about it. Until I have something to challenge the deputy coroner's findings, I really can't say that it's murder."

"OK, we can continue to listen to the gossip that flows in the arena. There's usually plenty of that. Now tell me about your trip to New Mexico."

Jonathon had spent three weeks with James Hernandez and his son on the ranch in northern New Mexico that had belonged to a mutual friend.

"I had a grand time. The place is beautiful, the mountains magnificent, and Jim and his family were very gracious hosts."

He then went on to fill me in on details of the trip and the misadventures of his flight there, where everything that could go wrong did.

"Well, it's getting late," he concluded, "and you have to be at the arena early, I know. So, I'll say good-night and be on my way."

I didn't argue with him because he was correct. I had to be out of here early the next morning and I was tired. We quickly moved the dishes from the table to the dishwasher and I walked him to the back porch.

"Drive carefully," I said, "and let me know if you learn anything that I should know."

"Will do, and that information track goes both ways."

"No problem." I watched as he got into his truck, turned around and gave a beep of his horn as he went through the gate. I followed him out and shut the outer gate so that the Pyrs could now be loose in this part of the property too. I could see them standing at the inner gate totally alert and waiting for me to let them out.

"Hi, guys. Ready to come in for the night?" I said as I opened the gate. I was answered by them taking off to check out the part of the yard that they had been kept out of during the day. With some quick marking of territory and a few warning barks, they were ready to come back to the house with me.

I finished cleaning up from dinner and continued to muse over Catalin's death. She was feisty and could be a pain in the butt, but people seemed to respect her in spite of it all. You don't usually kill those people you respect. So what had happened to turn someone into a killer? Was it done in the heat of a moment or had it been planned and calculated? I didn't have any answers and I was much too tired to worry about it any longer tonight. It was time for me to turn in, but before I did, I needed to run to the shop and get the book I had promised Dorothy Swanson.

The stars were bright when I walked out into the parking area that separated the house from the shop, and the moon was a lovely silver sliver just topping the horizon. I stopped for a moment just to watch and savor their beauty. I wasn't the best at picking out the various constellations, but I could usually find the Big Dipper and Orion if nothing else. As I stood there, Nali gave a bark and with Falcor close beside her raced toward the back fence. Then, over their challenge, I could hear the call of the coyotes. Looked like my dogs might be busy tonight.

Leaving them to their business, I continued on to the shop. I turned on the lights and did a quick walk through to make sure all was in order. Even after almost four years, I still marvel that this beautiful place is mine. The old barn on the property gave it a history and a beauty that couldn't be obtained with new structures. The main floor is divided by some of the old stall walls into focus areas for yarn, fiber, fiber equipment and a class room area. One of the stalls is blocked off with a picket fence to keep the dogs behind it but to allow them to be a part of what's going on. They have a dog door to enter it from the outside. The old wood stove remains to add supplemental heat in the winter and the ambience that only a wood stove can give. Around it, there is a sitting area for people to gather for knitting, spinning and conversation. Stairs go up the back wall to the old hay loft where I have the looms and store fleece and other supplies.

As I was looking for the book, I decided that I should also take a few more pattern books to the booth. Also, my latest copies of *Spin Off* had arrived so I gathered up a few of them to add to the booth shelves. After looking in some non-productive places, I found the book I was looking for, and with it and the other items in hand, I returned to the house and quickly to my bed. The dogs could take care of whatever needed to be done. I would sleep well knowing they were out there.

Chapter 13

After two beautiful days of spring sunshine, Saturday greeted us with northwest gray skies and a steady drizzle. That might be good for sales because people wouldn't be tempted to do outdoor activities. We'd just have to wait and see whether people opted for retail therapy or sitting at home by the fire.

There was already a line at the entrance to the fleece area when I walked into the arena and opened up my booth. This was always the busiest day of the Gathering because of the sale of fleeces that were high quality, clean, very well skirted and judged. And the good thing from a buyer's point of view was the fleece owner had to put the price on the fleece before it was judged. So sometimes you were able to get a beautiful, blue ribbon fleece for very little money per pound.

"Good morning," Ellen said as she came in through the door next to the Pyr booth. "I see you brought Nali again today."

"Yep, the coyotes were close and numerous last night. I decided that if there were even a chance that a dog might have to do more than make its presence known, it should be Falcor. Although Nali is doing very well, I have no desire to risk her getting injured again because she was not be up to the job requirements."

"Why didn't you just leave them both at home?"

"I thought about it, but this is the busiest day for you all too, and I figured another BWD might be a help."

"BWD?" asked a young man who had walked up to my booth. He was fairly tall with skin the color of cocoa and deep, dark eyes. There was a slight smile in them and on his lips as well.

"Big White Dog," I answered. "Shorthand for the Great Pyrenees, Kuvasz, Maremma and a few of the other white or mostly white livestock guardian dogs."

"Is that what she is?" he asked, indicating Nali.

"Yes, she is. She's a Great Pyrenees,as are the others that you see in the booth next to us. They're used to protect livestock from predators."

"She doesn't look all that fierce to me. Can she really take out a predator?"

"She can and has," I said. "It helps to have more than one if your predator load is heavy or something like a big cat."

"Is she friendly?"

"As long as she figures that you aren't any threat to Ellen or me or to her livestock. Her attitude can change in an instant if she senses any danger."

"May I pet her?

"Nali, do you want to get some pets?" Nali got up from where she was laying down and wandered over to the young man. She gave his outstretched hand a sniff and wagged her tail. "That was a good approach to a strange dog," I said as he slowly started scratching her chest.

"My mother showed dogs when I was small," he said. "She trained me well, but hers were a much smaller breed, Whippets."

"Great little dogs. I've thought of getting one from time to time. But can I help you with anything in the booth?"

"Actually, yes. I'm looking for a gift for my sister; her birthday is next week. She loves to knit, and I thought I might get her some yarn. I came because a friend of my mother's is supposed to have a booth here this weekend, but I didn't see it."

"What's her name?" I asked.

"This is silly, but I don't remember. I figured I'd just recognize her when I saw her. Oh well, I'm sure I can find something in your booth that will work."

"Well, let's see if we can."

I showed him a number of skeins of hand-painted yarn, some of which was handspun. After going back and forth over three different choices, he finally decided on two skeins of handspun in spring green tones that had a small amount of dog hair in it.

"I'm sure she'll like this," I said. "It should give her enough for a hat, a scarf, or a pair of socks. She might also be able to make a vest depending on the pattern."

"Oh, I think she'd like that. Would you have a pattern for a vest that would work with it?"

"I think so, let's look." I quickly checked the yardage requirements for a number of my vest patterns and came up with two possibles. "Either one of these would work."

"I like them both, and I don't know which one she might like. So I think I'll take both of them."

"A prudent choice. Here, I'll wrap them up for you and I'll put a business card in with it so she can call me if she has any questions."

"Thank you. Well, I better run. I still have other errands to do for my mother in town. I'll just have to tell her that I didn't see her friend. Bye, Nali," he added as he went out the door closest to us.

"Hmmm, I wonder if he was looking for Sheila." Ellen said from the Pyr booth where she'd been keeping track of us as she talked to various people.

"That's kind of stereotyping, isn't it?"

"Possibly, but it's also often true that our friends are those of our own race, and I wonder if it means that she still isn't at her booth."

"That's a good question. It would be worrisome if she weren't. I need to shop for my fleece," I added. "Can you keep an eye on things here and I'll check her booth as I come back from the fleece sale?"

The gate to the fleece had opened while I was busy at the booth and the area was already full of prospective buyers. I waved at Elizabeth Swanson, as I walked in and started down the rows of fleece. I quickly found the Corriedale that Dorothy Swanson had for sale. She was correct; it was a beautiful fleece with a blue ribbon, and she had put a reasonable price per pound on it. I picked it up and continued to look. Soon I found her Blue Faced Leicester. It too was gorgeous and went into my pile.

"What have you there?" Elizabeth asked as she came up.

"Two beautiful fleeces from your mother-in-law's sheep. She'd alerted me to them being here when I spoke to her earlier."

"How come she didn't tell me about them? Or even better, give me a chance to snag them before the show?" Elizabeth asked with a mock pout.

"Don't you have a birthday coming up soon? My guess is that she has one set aside for you as a birthday present."

"Hadn't thought of that," Elizabeth said and then added with a grin, "I guess I won't yell at her yet."

"I wouldn't. She's a pretty good resource to be related to if you're a spinner. Come though, let's look at the Romney fleece for you. It's an easy breed for a new spinner to work with, and I often find examples here that have a soft hand."

We began to go through the many Romney fleeces. They're a popular breed in our area because they can stand the wet weather.

"How about this one, Martha?" Elizabeth asked. "I love the color."

I looked at the judge's comments on the fleece that Elizabeth liked. It had received a blue ribbon and excellent marks by the judge and she'd also commented on the softness of the hand. I ran my hand over the fleece and looked closely at one of the staples. I carefully gathered up some of the fleece in my hand and gave it a squeeze. It was soft and had some bounce to it.

"I think it's an excellent choice, and the price is good too. I don't think you could go wrong by getting it."

"Then I will," she said. "I think one is enough for me, but they're all so lovely."

"They are lovely, but I agree. One is enough for you, especially since you have a source of fleece in the family if you decide you want to process a lot of them. I, however, need a couple more if I'm going to keep my stock up in my shop. Want to continue to shop with me?"

"I'd love to if you'll tell me what I'm looking at."

We continued to check out the fleece and I explained to Elizabeth what I was looking for and why I liked some fleece and not others. I didn't always agree with the judge when it came to my use for the fleece. I found the Shetland that Dorothy had alerted me to the day before and decided to get it, but the mohair was nowhere to be seen. That probably meant that it was in the silent auction.

When we finally finished, I had picked out two additional fleeces: a beautiful white Targhee and a lovely Jacob. Then as we were walking out, a lovely Romney caught my eye. It was a cream color, the hand was soft, and it was priced extremely well. I could sell it as raw fleece at the shop. So it was added to my growing pile.

By the time we got out of there, I decided that I would just take the fleece to my van. Then, realizing how long I'd been shopping, I decided I should at least call Ellen and see how she was doing.

"Are you lost?" she said as she answered her phone.

"No, but I ran into Elizabeth Swanson so the shopping trip turned into a teaching opportunity."

"I should have known. Well, it has been busy here, but nothing I can't handle. We had extra hands show up at the Pyr booth so they're doing OK without me."

"Good, then I'll take the fleeces to the van, go by Sheila's booth, and then come back to mine. I shouldn't be too long."

"See you soon."

I gathered up my fleeces and thought about checking for the mohair, but decided that could wait until later in the morning. The auction would be open until noon and by waiting, I might have a better idea of how high the fleece was going to go.

I headed out the door to the parking lot. The morning drizzle had turned to just gray for the moment, which made it easier to haul my load to the van. It didn't take me long to put the fleeces inside and lock it back up.

I retraced my steps to the arena and went straight to Sheila's booth. I didn't see Sheila although there were two women wandering within it looking at the various items. One had picked up some roving and looked like she was ready to make her purchase.

I looked over at Aloha, who was waiting on a customer at her booth. "Excuse me, Aloha, but have you seen Sheila?"

She glanced over at me. "Now that you mention it, I haven't. I've been so busy that I wasn't really paying any attention. Sandy, have you seen Sheila?" she asked the woman on the other side of Sheila's booth.

"Nope, I haven't. That seems strange. Most vendors really want to stay close on Saturday. It's the best day for sales."

"Can you just take my money?" asked the one woman. "I have the correct amount and I really want to get to the fleece sale."

"Sure," I said. I took the woman's money and looked for a bag to put her roving into.

"That's OK," she said. "I can just put it into my backpack."

"OK, enjoy your roving."

The second woman walked out with her, so evidently they were together. I looked for a place to put the money for Sheila and found her cash box underneath one of her tables. I put the money away and then decided to take it with me. I'd give it to Rex; there was a fair amount of money in it, and it didn't seem a good idea to leave it there. I also noticed that she had some sheets under the table. She probably used them to cover her tables when she shut down for the night.

"I'm going to take her cash box and give it to Rex," I said, "and I'm going to cover her wares with a sheet. It should keep people out of her booth until we can figure out where she's gotten to."

"Thanks," Aloha said. "I'm much too busy to have to worry about her booth today."

"No problem. I'll give Rex a call when I get back to my booth and alert him to the fact that she seems to be missing."

I took Sheila's cash box and walked quickly back to my own booth. Ellen would be ready to shoot me.

"Here she is," Ellen said. "This woman has a question about your handspun that I can't answer."

"How can I help you?" I asked. She was holding a skein of my hand-painted yarn.

"I want to use this to trim a white shawl. Is the dye fast?"

"I work very hard to make sure that it is," I said. "But you might want to rinse the skein again to make sure. If you get any dye runoff, you are welcome to bring the skein back to me. I sure wouldn't want it to harm your white shawl."

"OK, I'll do that," she said.

I wrapped up her skein and took her money. "I've put a business card in with your yarn. If you have any problems, be sure to contact me."

"I will. Thanks for your help."

All of a sudden, I had a rush of customers. Then I heard someone say that they had come on a bus with other members of their spinning guild. They were from Vancouver and also planned on going to Shipwreck Beads, north of Olympia, this afternoon before heading back down south. That would explain the large number of people at one time. I was just finishing up with a customer when her friend walked up.

"Is there any place here to get food?"

"There's a food area set up in one of the out buildings," I said. "I know that the Boy Scouts have burgers, Black Hills Café has a booth, and there is a booth with chili. If you go out this door, you'll see signs pointing you in that direction."

"Thanks, I'm starved." She turned and headed toward the door and then stopped for a couple of minutes to talk to the Pyrs in the club booth before going on out.

Chapter 14

"Whew," I said to Ellen. "We don't usually get our people in such quick succession."

"I know. We didn't get hit quite so bad. It would have been different if it had been a busload of children. But tell me, what did you find out about Sheila?"

"Oh, I'd forgotten in the rush of customers. No one has seen her this morning. I have her cash box with me and I need to get it to Rex. I'd better call him," I added as I pulled out my cell phone.

"Rex, this is Martha Williamson. Have you seen Sheila today? Did she say anything to you about coming in late or not coming in at all?"

"Isn't she at her booth?"

"No and the women on either side of her haven't seen her. I took her cash box and covered her stuff with sheets, but it seems very odd that she isn't here. I know she was worried about making ends meet this month. She sure can't help that by not being here to sell her stuff."

"I'll call around and see what I can find out."

"Please do that and then come by and get the money. I'd much rather have it locked up in your office than here in my booth."

"Will do. I'll be by in a few minutes."

"That really is odd," Ellen said. "Most vendors hardly leave their booths to go to the bathroom if they don't have backup like somebody I know."

"And I can't tell you how much that backup is appreciated. I seem to be making more use of it than usual this year."

"Well, we usually don't have someone killed on the premises. I'm assuming that Jonathon now thinks it's murder."

I filled her in on my conversation with Jonathon the night before and finished up just as I saw Rex headed my way.

"So did you talk to her?" I asked.

"No and I tried both her cell phone and the trailer where she is living right now. It does seem very odd."

"There you are, Rex, I've been looking all over for you. Have you seen Sheila?" A small gray-haired woman with skin the color of chestnuts and soft brown eyes came from the direction of Sheila's booth. "I was supposed to meet up with her after I picked up my fleece today. Her booth is covered with sheets. Why would she do that?"

"Actually, I covered it with sheets when I found people wandering among her stock and she was nowhere to be found," I said. "I didn't want her things to be stolen."

"But where is Sheila? Her car is in the parking lot. She must be here someplace."

"Her car is in the lot?" Rex asked. "Oh, Martha, this is Charlotte Dubois. Charlotte, this is Martha Williamson."

"That's what I said, wasn't it? Good to meet, you Martha. Thank you for taking care of Sheila's booth. But, Rex, the point is Sheila is missing and her car is in the lot."

"It was there all night, Rex." This came from one of the sheep ranchers who was talking to Ellen at the Pyr booth and obviously also listening to our conversation. "I just figured that she'd decided to bed down here rather than do the long drive home."

"If she'd done that, she would have been at her booth early this morning," I said.

"I think it's time to start looking for her in earnest," Rex said. "Come on Martha, Charlotte, let's spread out over the grounds and see what we can find."

I looked at Ellen.

"Yep, I'll take over. You and Nali go see if you can find her."

I leashed Nali and followed Rex and Charlotte out the door closest to us into what was now a rather steady downpour.

"Martha, you take the two stables that have animals from the Gathering in them. Charlotte, would you go down to the food area and the storage building that is closest to it? I'll take the stables that aren't part of the Gathering and shouldn't have anyone from it in them."

Charlotte and I agreed and headed for our assigned locations.

"OK, Nali girl, you can hear and smell much better than I can so you need to help me out with this."

We walked into one end the nearest stable. I stopped for a minute to let my eyes become accustomed to the darker building, then Nali and I started down the row of stalls. We passed by a lot of sheep. Some of them seemed to be familiar with big white dogs and hardly gave Nali a second glance. Others moved to the back of the stalls, obviously not sure about her, even though Nali was walking slowly and easily and making no movement in their direction.

"Hey, Dorothy," I said as I came up to her stall area, "have you seen Sheila Barnes? She hasn't been at her booth this morning, and no one has seen her, but her car is in the lot."

"Last I saw her was sometime yesterday. Want me to help look?"

"I don't think we need you yet. There are three of us looking, but if we decide we need reinforcements, I'll call you. By the way, I did snag two of your lovely fleeces."

"I'm glad. I was sure you would like the Corriedale. Which other one did you get?"

"The BFL. It's a beautiful specimen of the breed. And as a hint, I hope you have a nice one set aside for Elizabeth for her birthday. She's getting addicted."

Dorothy chuckled. "You do create monsters, don't you, my friend. Yep, I actually have two for her. One is a lovely bluish shade of gray and the other is a white so you can teach her to dye."

"More work for me. But I'll love it. Well, I better get searching."

"Let me know when you find her."

"Will do," I said as I continued down the row.

I made it to the end of that aisle and went out the door at the end and then back in the door next to it that took me down the second aisle. Still no Sheila.

"Well, Nali, we've checked this one. Let's go next door."

We moved to the next stable and I noticed that it was arranged differently. There weren't as many stalls and there were some closed areas with doors. Maybe tack rooms or other storage areas. There was also a set of stairs that went up to a loft area. Nali and I went up the stairs; there were bales of hay at one end.

"Nali, go check them out," I said and let go of her leash. She went all around them and climbed up on the ones that she could. Her nose went into every crevice and I could see her ears twitching as she listened for anything among the bales. While she was searching, I went over to the rail that ran along the edge of the loft. It gave me a pretty good view of all the stalls and I couldn't see anyone in any of them. I'd double check when Nali and I got back down there, but I had a feeling that we'd come up with a zero here too. After a bit, she came back to me and sat. Obviously she was wondering what I wanted her to find.

"Good job, big girl. Let's go back downstairs."

We went down the stairs and started down the row of stalls. There were a few sheep and about half a dozen llamas but no people in any of them. I'd about given up but we still hadn't checked the closed rooms. They'd probably be locked, but I needed to check. As I turned toward the closest one, Nali stopped.

"What is it, girl? Show me."

She started toward one of the closed doors and nosed it when she got there. I tried the knob. Locked. I listened, but couldn't hear anything. However, Nali was still very interested in it. Time to call Rex.

"Rex, can you come to the stable with the loft and storage rooms? Oh and bring your master key with you. Nali thinks she's found something."

"I'm on my way."

I crouched down and gave Nali a pet. "Good job, big girl."

Rex came into the stable at a trot. He had obviously been

outside more than I had because his hair was plastered against his head and his jacket was dripping from the rain. "What did you find?"

"I don't know. It may be nothing, but Nali thinks we should check this room."

Rex put his master key in the lock and opened the door. The aroma of leather and wax and saddle soap wafted out. This was obviously a tack room. It was also dark, too dark to see anything. Just as I found a light switch, I heard a moan, and Nali let out a whine and dashed into the room. With the lights on, both Rex and I could see Sheila sprawled on the floor facedown with her dog next to her. Nali whined and nosed Sheila. Again we heard a soft moan. She was alive. Rex reached for his cell phone and I squatted down next to her.

"It's OK, Sheila, we've found you."

Once I was next to Sheila, Nali moved over to the dog. She sniffed it; looked up at me and then just sat next to it. I figured that was a good signal that the dog was dead.

"They're on their way," Rex said, then turned as we both heard footsteps in the stable. Looking at me first, he went to the door to see who it was.

"We don't need visitors," he said over his shoulder to me, but then on seeing our intruder, stepped aside to let the person in the room.

"What's happening, Martha, Rex?" Mark said as he walked into the tack room.

"We've found Sheila, but she's seriously injured," I said.

Mark knelt down next to her and began to look her over. There were slashes in the back of her blouse and significant blood stains. At least part or maybe all of her injuries were there. The blood had also started to dry so these weren't recent injuries.

"Here, Martha, help me loosen her blouse from her jeans and see if I can lift it up to see just what's happened here. I don't want to injure her worse or cause her any more pain if I can help it."

I reached down on my side of Sheila and Mark and I began to gently pull her blouse up and out of her jeans. She moaned again very softly.

"You hang in there, Sheila, you hear? Help's on its way."

Mark had gotten her blouse about halfway up her back and I could see the deep gash. It did not appear to be the only one either. Mark was just starting to increase the opening in the blouse where the slashes were when we heard the sirens.

"Guess I'll leave this for the experts," he said. "They'll have the equipment to do things right."

And as he finished his sentence two medics rushed in the stable door with another right behind them pushing a gurney.

"Over here," Rex said. "She's inside the tack room."

They came in and knelt beside her.

"You didn't turn her over?" One of them directed the question to Mark.

"No, I didn't want to risk greater injury."

The medic just nodded and started checking Sheila's vital signs. "Her pulse is weak, but it's there. Her blood pressure is also low, but she's obviously a strong young woman, because from the looks of things, she's been here awhile."

He too looked at the gash that we'd uncovered and then reached into his kit and took out a pair of scissors, which he used to cut the blouse and reveal the rest of her back. There were three more knife wounds.

"How did she survive those?" I asked.

"I don't know," the medic said, "but I think the quicker we get her to the hospital the better."

"I think Jonathon's going to want to see her in place first," I said.

"Then he better get here, because I want to get her to medical treatment."

"Here he is," Rex said as we heard footsteps outside the door.

"What's happening?" Jonathon asked as he stepped through the door and then he saw Sheila. "Damn. Who found her?"

"Nali did," I said. "At least she alerted me that there was something amiss in the room. I called Rex because the door was locked and the three of us came in together. Rex put in the call to emergency as soon as we saw her on the floor. Mark came in shortly after that. We had started looking for her when everyone realized that she hadn't gone home last night and wasn't around this morning."

"So this may have happened yesterday?"

"From the looks of her wounds, I'd say so," the medic joined in, "and I'd like to get her to the hospital if you'll let me move her."

"Let me take a couple of quick pictures so I have her in place and then you can."

Jonathon got out his camera and took pictures of Sheila and the room from a number of different angles. He then paced off the room so he had at least a general idea of where she was laying.

"OK, guys, you can move her. I'll call in help to go over the crime scene."

"Let's get her moved to the gurney," the medic said. "You want to help us?" He directed this last to Mark.

Mark nodded his agreement and moved into position to help the three medics move Sheila.

"On the count of three—one, two, three."

The men carefully lifted Sheila and placed her on the gurney.

"Do we want to turn her over?" the medic who had brought in the gurney asked.

The other man thought a minute. He was obviously the senior member of the crew. He then nodded. Again the men got in place and gently lifted her up and turned her over onto her back. Again she moaned and her eyes started to open and then closed. She had a bruise and scrape on her left cheek that might have come from her fall to the floor of the tack room. Other than that, there were no obvious wounds on the front of her.

"Let's get her out of here."

Just as they started out, I heard running footsteps.

"What's happened? I saw the emergency vehicles. Oh, please tell me it's not Sheila!"

"I'm sorry, Charlotte," Rex said, "but it is Sheila and she's been seriously injured."

"Injured? How? Let me see her."

Before the medic could stop her, Charlotte pushed her way to the side of the gurney. Her face paled and her mouth set in a firm line.

"What in hell happened here? What's going on at this Gathering, Rex?"

"We don't know what happened, but Sheila was attacked," Jonathon answered for Rex, "and it's important that for now you don't talk to people about it."

"I must call her mother. She must be told."

"I will do that," Jonathon said.

She looked at Jonathon, then back at Sheila. Nodding her head in a decisive manner, she looked at the medic.

"I'll follow you to the hospital. Let's go."

"Fine with me. Let's get going," the medic said to his men.

I watched as they wheeled the gurney out of the tack room and then out of the stable with Charlotte by Sheila's side. Jonathon was on his phone when I turned around and walked back into the tack room.

"OK, get here as quick as you can," he said as he hung up and looked toward Rex, Mark and me. "OK, now fill me in again with a few more details, please."

Rex and I told him what we knew of Sheila's actions based on what we had gleaned before we went looking for her.

"So the last anyone saw her that you know of was when she asked Aloha to look after her booth yesterday afternoon."

"That's correct. I didn't go back down there later yesterday and I guess that the other women were busy enough that they didn't really think about it. I didn't get worried until I found out that she wasn't there again this morning. And we really got worried when we learned that her car was in the lot and had been there all night. That's when we started searching the other buildings."

Jonathon looked down at Nali, who was still sitting beside the dead dog. "Looks like you're our number one detective on this case, Nali."

At the sound of her name, she got up and walked over to Jonathon, where she sat in front of him. He started scratching her ears. "Good girl."

Mark got up from where he had been examining the dog. "It looks like she was killed with a blow to the head instead of a knife," he said. "I can do a necropsy if you want me to."

"Please do, Mark, and fax me your findings as quickly as you can."

"I can do it this afternoon."

"Thanks. OK, Rex and Martha, you can go back to whatever you need to do. My men will be here soon and we can handle things here. I know where to find you and I have your cell numbers if I need you. Oh and don't start spreading rumors. If people ask about Sheila, just say she was injured and has been taken to the hospital."

Rex nodded and headed for the door. I waited for Mark as he bent down over the still form of the small black dog. I knew that this was hurting him far more than he was letting on. The unnecessary death of an animal always got to him. Nali must have known too because she gently bumped his arm with her nose and then gave his ear a snuffle just before he rose back up with the dog in his arms.

"I'll walk to your van with you," I said, "and why were you here this morning anyway?"

"I'd come to see if you wanted company for lunch. Ellen said you were out searching the buildings for Sheila so I headed in this direction in case I could be of help. I was just lucky in that I chose the correct stable to check first."

"Well, I'm glad you came. It was good to have you here, especially before the medics came."

We had arrived at Mark's van, and I opened the back doors for him.

"Get me one of those blankets so I can wrap this girl up."

I reached in and pulled a clean blanket from a pile that was on one side of the van and opened it up on the floor. Mark gently lay the dog onto it, wrapped her up and shut the back doors.

"Since we missed lunch, how about supper?" he asked.

"Shall we pick up pizza and just take it to my place? I doubt that I will want to get cleaned up to go out anywhere?"

"That will work for me."

"OK, come by about seven o'clock and I should be ready to go. Or do you just want to meet me at my place about seven forty-five?"

"Why don't I get the pizza and come directly to your place?"

"You got a date. Well, Ellen will think I've completely deserted her again. I'm going to owe her big time for this Gathering. I think she's worked my booth more than I have."

I gave him a long hug and Nali and I walked back toward the arena. Who had killed Sheila's dog and tried to kill her? The obvious answer was the person that had killed Catalin. But who was that, and why kill Sheila? Had she seen something or said something that led the person to believe that she knew their identity? Lots of questions and no answers. It was turning into a very long Fiber Gathering.

Chapter 15

Ellen was swamped when I got back. She had three customers in my booth and one of the Pyr people was asking her a question in order to get an answer to a visitor's
query.

"OK, I can take over here," I said as I walked up. She gave
me a grateful look and moved over to the Pyr booth to help out
there.

Two of the people in my booth appeared to be just browsing. The other, a young woman with red and purple dye inter-
mingled with her natural brown, short-spiked hair and multiple
piercings on her ears and face had two different books in her
hands. She appeared to be having a problem deciding on one,
both or neither.

"Can I help you?" I asked.

"I hope so. I'm a pretty new spinner and I thought one of
these might help me improve, but I can't decide on which one."

I looked at the books. She was holding *The Intentional Spinner* by Judith Mackenzie McCuin and *Spin Control* by Amy King.

"Both are excellent, and each has its own strengths," I said. "Amy King gives you a rundown of the different kinds of wheels, Judith really doesn't cover them. Judith spends a lot more time on the different types of fiber. About one-third of her book covers that. She also has projects in the back of her book and instructions on how to spin for each particular project. Both books cover the difference between worsted and woolen well. Both cover the basics of different kinds of yarn that you can spin. Judith's book is a little more expensive than Amy's, but it has more pages."

"I kind of figured that out by looking at them," she said with some frustration in her voice, "but I still don't know which one to buy and I can only afford one."

"OK, then I'll give you my opinion on which one I would buy. I would buy Judith's. Not because if you buy it, you are buying the more expensive book, but because I happen to really like Judith's teaching style. She's opinionated, but she usually has good reasons for her opinions. I always learn something from her wherever I happen to see her. I love to watch her judge fleece and I've learned a lot from her on choosing fleece and the properties of fleece by being in the audience when she is judging."

"OK, I'll take this one," she said and handed me the copy of Judith's book. She then placed the other one carefully back on the shelf where it belonged. I love considerate shoppers.

"I think you'll enjoy it," I said. "There's a lot in there to learn and practice. By the way, you're welcome to come by the shop to spin. I give private lessons, but don't require you to take them to get answers to questions. A lot of my customers just stop by awhile for the company, a comfortable place to spin and a cup of coffee. And every Thursday at noon, there are a bunch of women who come by to knit, spin or crochet depending on their preference at the time."

"I think I'd like that. I just moved here in January to start the winter quarter at Evergreen so I don't know a whole lot of fiber people here. My name is Angelic Denato."

"I'm Martha Williamson. I'll put a business card in with your book. Call me if you have any questions or need directions to the shop. Also from time to time, one of our Thursday people is a professor from Evergreen, Michael Green."

"Oh, I know Professor Green. I didn't know he was interested in fiber. Maybe I could even catch a ride with him. I'll have to ask. Thanks again for your help," she said and, gathering up her package, she moved down the aisle of vendors.

"Now tell me what happened," Ellen asked as she wandered over from the Pyr booth.

I filled her in on what had happened to Sheila and her dog.

"What kind of bastard would kill a dog?"

"I think the dog was used to lure Sheila into the tack room," I answered. "My guess is that when she walked into the tack room her only concern was for her dog there on the floor and she didn't even notice her attacker."

"You're probably right. I'm sure in the same circumstances I would be focused only on my dog."

"Me too."

I glanced at my watch. I would just have time to check on the silent auction. Did I dare ask Ellen to take over again? I looked up at her.

"Now what do you want to do? I can tell that look."

"Well, I can just get one bid in on that mohair at the silent auction if I go right now."

"Go. Nali and I can hold down the fort here."

"Thanks."

I took off across the arena to the fleece sales area. The silent auction fleeces were set out on tables in a section fenced off from the rest of the fleece.

"You better hurry. We close in three minutes," one of the volunteers said.

"Will do, I'm just interested in the mohair."

However, I still had to look at all of the fleeces. They really were beautiful. Our shepherds were doing a grand job of producing quality fleece for spinners. I spotted the mohair, and Dorothy was right. It really was lovely. It was a small fleece and would provide just what I needed to blend with other fiber for my handspun.

"One minute to closing," the volunteer said.

Quite a few people were hovering around the fleece that they wanted waiting until the last second to put in their bid, but no one in the area seemed to be interested in the mohair. I picked up the pen beside the bid sheet and added my bid at the bottom. Only three other people had placed bids on it.

"Bidding is closed. Please step out of the fleece area." The volunteer walked in and ushered the four of us that were left out of the enclosure.

"I hate to pull rank, but I need to get back to my booth. Do you think you could process the mohair fleece first?" I asked the volunteer at the payment table. She was a shepherd that I was acquainted with from previous Gatherings.

"Sure thing, Martha. Janet, would you hand me the mohair? You really got a bargain on this lovely fluff," she added as she received the fleece.

"I did. I have Dorothy Swanson to thank for that. She alerted me to it's presence and quality."

"Dorothy has a great eye for fleece, and she did well in the judging too."

"She did and I picked up a couple of her blue ribbon fleeces earlier. They will be a joy to work with."

"Your total is thirty-seven eighty with the tax."

I quickly wrote her a check and gathered up my parcel.

"Good luck with the rest of the sales. Looks like you could be done with all of the fleece by this evening from the empty space on the tables."

"We will be, I'm sure. Thanks again for your support."

I waved and quickly made my way back to my booth.

"Thanks again," I said to Ellen as I entered the booth.

"No problem, you weren't terribly busy and the Pyr booth has plenty of help right now. I was even thinking of getting some food. Can I pick up anything for you?"

"You going to the Black Hills Café booth?"

"Yep, want some soup?"

"I do."

"OK, want me to take Nali?"

"Want to go with Ellen, Nali?"

In answer, she got up and walked over to Ellen.

"I guess that's a yes. See both of you in a few minutes."

I kept busy with the sale of a couple of spindles and some roving while I waited, and then I caught sight of them coming through the door. Nali preceded Ellen past the Pyr booth and into mine, looking very proud of herself as she carried a large rawhide bone in her mouth.

"And where did you get that?" I asked as I looked at her. She answered by settling down at the back of the booth with her prize nestled between her front paws.

"Rex gave it to her. We ran into him outside. He was heading this way with it. He told her that she deserved a steak but would have to settle for this. I'm not sure where he had it hiding."

"Probably he has some stashed to give to the herding demonstration dogs when they're done." One of the highlights for visitors to the Gathering was the demonstration of their skills by the herding dogs. Children especially enjoyed it.

"I hadn't thought about that. You're probably right. Anyway, she said thank you nicely and took her bone like the lady that she is."

"Glad to learn that she remembered her manners. However, if you don't give me my soup, I might lose mine. It smells wonderful and I'm ravenous. What did you get?"

"Broccoli and cheese. I also got a piece of Sally's bread for each of us."

We were having a lull so we decided to sit in my booth while we enjoyed our soup. As Sally's food always is, it was excellent; and we ate in silence for a bit.

"Have you gotten any work done on Donovan's Web site or has the Gathering stopped all work?

"You know me. I'm a night owl; so yes, I have gotten some work done on it. The basic pages are outlined and I've placed some pictures on a couple of them. I need to contact him and see if he likes the direction I'm going before I do much more. That may have to wait until after the Gathering. We'll see."

"I don't know how you manage to work here and do anything else. By the time I get home, I just want to put my feet up and collapse. Whichever dog is here with me feels the same way. I can't imagine getting anything productive done in the evening."

"Ah, but unlike you, the evening and night are my most productive times. What's hard is getting here in time to open up in the morning. Thank goodness, I don't have to do that tomorrow."

"True. Well, my bowl is empty. Want me to dump this trash?"

"I'll do it. I see people who look like fiber junkies coming our way."

I looked down the aisle and saw quite a few women with tote bags and bags of fleece in their hands.

"I think you might be correct."

The next couple of hours were busy. I answered questions, demonstrated both the wheels and the loom, and actually sold quite a few items including one rigid heddle loom that the woman would pick up at the shop next Tuesday. I'd offered to set it up and put it on the stand that she had also purchased. She'd jumped at the chance to not have to deal with "some assembly required."

I'd just finished handing a woman her purchase when I saw Ellen look toward the main arena doors.

"Uh oh. Here comes trouble."

I followed her gaze and grimaced.

"You're right about that, and he looks like a man with a mission." Catalin's brother was walking toward our end of the building and he did not look happy.

"Where's that Rex Meredith?" he said as he stormed up to my booth.

"Good afternoon, Mr. Ezkarra. I haven't seen Rex since late this morning. He may be in the stables. Can I help you with anything?"

"I want to get Catalin's animals now and some lackey says that I can't."

"That's correct. Animals can't be removed from the arena or the stables until the end of the Gathering."

"That's ridiculous. She's dead. Do you mean to tell me that you people can hold her animals hostage and not let the rightful owner remove them?"

"Well, those are the rules. I imagine that Rex could make an exception for the rightful owner, but I don't believe that you're that person."

"You what?"

"I said that I don't believe that you own Catalin's animals."

"What do you mean? I'm her brother and her closest living relative."

"That may be true, but I believe that her will leaves all of her property to someone else and that would include her livestock."

"Her will does what? That's ridiculous. She doesn't have anyone else to leave it to. Well, that no good son of mine, but I'm sure she wouldn't be that stupid."

"I suggest that you talk to her attorney, Mr. Ezkarra; but the rumor I've heard is that the will stipulates another person as the recipient of her property."

"Did she actually leave it to that brown bitch? Was she vengeful enough to actually throw her lifestyle in my face at her death and leave it to her?"

"I suggest that you talk to her attorney."

"You bet I will. If she thought that she could continue to desecrate God's laws even in her death, I have news for everyone. That union was sinful and not legal. I can't believe that any such disposition of her property would stand up in court."

"Well, as I said, you need to talk to her attorney or yours. In the meantime, her animals will remain at the Gathering until at least tomorrow. Then I'm sure Rex will talk to her attorney to decide what's to be done with them. My guess is they'll just be returned to her ranch. People are taking care of the animals there until things shake out."

"Obviously none of you people have any respect for God or His laws. I'm just glad that my parents' estate wasn't settled yet. They'd be turning over in their grave if they even thought that their money would go to that heathen."

"Well, I'm sure they knew of Catalin's living arrangement when they left her half of their money."

"They did, but Catalin was their daughter. They weren't going to cut her out of the will. However, there is a six-month provision in the will. Since Catalin didn't live six months after my parents' death, all of the money comes to me. None of it goes into Catalin's estate and none of it will go to whomever she was dumb enough to leave her ranch and money."

"Is that significant?" I asked.

"You betcha it's significant. I got my business acumen from my father. His father came to this country from Spain a poor shepherd, but my father made his fortune, and now Catalin's sins will not be rewarded with their money. It'll come to me."

"Well, I'm sure that you and your attorney will sort everything out. I think I see Rex coming this way if you still want to talk to him."

"He'll just give me the same garbage you did, I'm sure. I'm not going to waste my time with you people anymore. My attorney will be calling him. Just make sure that nothing happens to those valuable animals."

With that he turned on his heel and barreled out the door next to the Pyr booth.

"That was some tantrum," Ellen said.

"Yes, and it looks to me like he had a great motive for wanting to see his sister dead."

"Sounded like two to me," Ellen added. "He hated her guts because she didn't follow his interpretation of God's laws and he's going to inherit a whole bunch more money since she died before the six months were up."

"Makes me wonder if he felt that he was the chosen one to administer God's justice in Catalin's case."

"Was that Joseba Ezkarra?" Rex asked as he walked up. "What did he want? I'm sure it was only to make problems."

"He wanted to take Catalin's animals and was furious that someone told him he couldn't," I answered. "He was looking for you, but I took the brunt of his wrath for you."

"Sorry that happened, Martha, but I won't deny that I have no desire to talk to him."

"No problem. I just told him that no animals could be moved until the end of the Gathering. I also told him that they'd be given to the person who was the rightful owner, and I wasn't sure that he was that person."

"Oh boy, I bet that set him off."

"It did. I just told him to talk to her attorney or to his. He wasn't happy as you could see by the way he exited the building."

"Well, I came by to let you know that Jonathon has finished up in the stable and will be coming through here talking to the various vendors."

"I assume that he'll start with those closest to her booth."

"Probably, and I imagine he'll finish with you since he pretty well knows what you think."

"Are you going to pack up her booth, Rex?"

"I guess I should. I'll have to see if I can find any boxes."

"I think you'll find the plastic bins that she used to bring things here under some of her tables. I saw some when I was looking for her cash box."

"Thanks. I guess I'll go there now, and if there are enough bins, I can just get it done."

"I'll help you out with that, Rex," Ellen said. "If I don't, Martha'll volunteer and I'll be stuck taking care of her booth again."

I laughed. "Off with you two then. Ellen, keep your eyes open for anything unusual."

As they headed back down the aisle toward Sheila's booth, I noticed a woman at the Pyr booth who was looking at me in a rather quizzical way. She was about my height with lots of frizzy red hair framing a round face and with the weathered skin of someone who spent a lot of time outdoors. Her eyes were a beautiful green. I'd guess that she had been a real beauty in her youth. Even now, and with the puzzlement on her face, she was attractive.

"Can I help you?"

"What? No, well, maybe. It's just that the nasty man who was just yelling at you seems familiar. I could swear that I saw him get out of a car late on Wednesday. I was just leaving after making sure that my animals were all settled for the night. It took me longer than usual because one lamb came up lame, and I had to talk to Rex to get permission to take him home. Anyway, a man drove in quickly and parked in a manner that took up two parking spots. He got out of his car, slammed the door and took off at almost a sprint toward the stables. It might have been the same man, but it was almost dark so I'm not totally sure. Do you think I should tell someone?"

"It wouldn't hurt to tell Police Chief Green. He's here at the

Gathering and should be in the arena soon if he isn't already. You might check down closer to the main entrance. The name of the man you saw talking to me is Joseba Ezkarra. You can just tell Jonathon the same thing you told me; then he can take it from there if he thinks it's important."

"Thank you. I'll do that. My name, by the way, is Loreena Cameron. I have a small farm outside of Elma."

"I'm Martha Williamson, Loreena. It's good to meet you."

"Well, I better go find Chief Green, but I'd like to come back and talk to you later about spinning and Great Pyrenees if I might."

"Absolutely, there are no other subjects that I like to talk about more. If you don't make it during the Gathering, here's my card. Come by the shop or call me."

"I'll do that."

I turned from watching her leave and moved back into my booth. Could she have seen Joseba? If so, it meant that he too was in a position to kill Catalin. The first time he was at the Gathering was not the morning she was found and we had our first confrontation with him, but the night before. That could turn any suppositions that Jonathon had upside down. He sure seemed to have a nasty enough temper to have hit her in a fit of rage or maybe even done something more calculating. And since he seemed to be in the area for the weekend, there was no reason why he couldn't have come onto the grounds and attempted to kill Sheila. He sure hated her enough. Maybe he should move to the top of the suspect list. Something I would have to think about.

Chapter 16

I decided to pull out my spinning wheel to occupy my time until someone needed my help. I was just getting started when I heard footsteps behind me and Nali jumped up with her tail going a mile a minute. Since Ellen had recently walked away in the opposite direction, it could only be one of two people. Mark was busy at the clinic, so I figured it was my brother.

"Hey, Sean," I said without turning around.

"Got eyes in the back of your head like Mom?"

"Nope, Nali told me. She only greets three people like that and I know where the other two are right now."

"Hey, Nali girl," he said with a laugh, "you gave me away."

Nali figured that was an invitation to get pets and ear scritches so she ambled over to Sean. Of course, she was correct; he squatted down and gave her a good rubbing all over.

"So what brings you here?"

"I just came off shift and decided to drop in and see how you were doing. Also thought you might be able to update me on the thing with Catalin Ezkarra. I saw something at the station about an accidental death. I could have called Jonathon, but figured you'd probably know all the scoop since you were here."

Sean had recently been promoted to detective in the Thurston County Sheriff's Office and had good friends in and maintained good relationships with the Black Hills Police Department.

"Well, to begin with I'm sure that the accidental death label has been changed to murder," I said and then went on to fill him in on all the details that I knew in the case.

"I've met Catalin," he said. "She was quite a tiger when you angered her. I've been called out to her property for vandalism at least once and some hate crime graffiti once. We never did catch either perpetrator, which didn't please her."

"I imagine that it didn't, but that kind of crime is very hard to solve."

"Pretty much impossible, unless you catch them in the act. Anyway, I can see her getting on the wrong side of someone, but to the point of murder......"

"Well, it happened this time," I said. "I have a mental list of suspects; all of whom have motive and probably opportunity, but none of whom, except her brother, seem to be likely candidates. And I'm probably excepting her brother just because I really don't like the man."

"Well, being a nice person doesn't exempt someone from murder, especially if it was done in a fit of rage or to defend oneself, and I could see someone needing to defend themselves from Catalin if she were really angry."

"I know. That's what keeps Rex on my list. She was furious with him and they had two very loud and heated arguments here on Wednesday. I could see her coming at him and him needing to defend himself. What I don't understand from that scenario is the cover-up. And that also doesn't help with explaining the attempted murder of Sheila. Why go after her if the killing of Catalin was done in the heat of anger? And, of course, the attack on Sheila kind of removes her from my original list."

"The murderer may have thought that she knew something," Sean replied. "And I'm not sure that it totally removes her from the original list. What if Sheila did the murder and then someone else who thought they would inherit realized that Sheila would get the estate? They might then go after Sheila where they wouldn't have gone after Catalin. Both the nephew and brother could fall into that category."

"Hmm, hadn't looked at it that way. Guess it does give another way to consider things."

"By the way, what did you say Catalin's nephew's name is?"

"Kelmen Ezkarra. Why?"

"It kind of rings a bell with me, and I'm wondering why. What does he look like?"

"About my height, stocky but not overly heavy, very dark hair and eyes, a Mediterranean skin tone, actually fairly good looking from a woman's point of view."

"Now I remember; I pulled him over just this side of the Red Wind Casino on the Yelm highway. He was speeding and not too happy with the world. Made some crack about the blankety-blank Indians setting up speed traps. Needless to say that comment didn't make me want to issue just a warning. My guess is he'd lost money that night at the casino."

"Hmm, Ellen and I saw him at the Sky Mountain Casino on Thursday night. At least we're pretty sure it was him. He denied being there when I asked him about it. But he wasn't happy that night either. I suppose gambling debts could be a motive for murder, especially if you thought you would inherit a large sum of money."

"It could. Well, I need to get back into town. You take warning from what happened to Sheila. Obviously, whoever killed Catalin is willing to do it again. They won't be happy with you putting your nose into things. Leave it to the professionals."

"Yes, little brother. I promise, I won't go digging, but I will keep my eyes and ears open."

"Figured that I couldn't stop you from that."

I gave him a hug and watched as he left by the closest door. Was Kelmen a compulsive gambler? Could he owe money that he couldn't pay? If he were gambling at the casinos, might he be gambling at places where the people weren't as nice? Then I got an idea.

I pulled my cell phone out of my pocket and dialed.

"Hey, I was just thinking of you. Ready to quit for the day?" Mark said.

"Don't I wish. I've got a little over an hour to go. Would you do me a favor?"

"Anytime. What do you need?"

"I need some information from the Indian casinos and I thought the people there might be more apt to talk to you. You wouldn't happen to know any of the staff at one or more of them, would you?"

"I do know the manager at Sky Mountain. He and I were at WSU at the same time. I'll call him and see if I can find anything out for you. What do you want to know?"

I explained what I was trying to find out about Kelmen.

"Well, he might not have that kind of info, but maybe he can get it from someone who works the floor. I'll ask him."

"Thank you so much. See you tonight,"

"Looking forward to it. What kind of pizza do you want?"

"As long as it has pepperoni and sausage, I'm OK with it."

"OK, will get those two at least. Probably get a meat combo."

"Sounds good. See ya."

I hung up smiling. It would be good to spend some time with Mark this evening. The next thirty minutes went by quickly as one customer after another stopped by the booth. It was going to be a good day for sales in spite of me leaving Ellen in charge so much this morning. And as if thinking of her could produce her, Ellen walked in the side door.

"Well, we have all of her stuff packed into her bins and the bins stored in Rex's office under lock and key. It took us a little longer than I expected because Jonathon wanted to go over the booth first."

"I didn't think of that possibility, but I guess it makes sense."

"I don't think he found anything. At least, he didn't take anything with him. She had some nice fiber, though. My guess is it was from their sheep. I'd have been interested in purchasing some if things had worked out differently."

"She might appreciate the purchases later. I'm sure that money'll be short for awhile and who knows when the estate stuff will get settled? Joseba's going to make it difficult for her. You can count on that."

"You have a point there. I picked up a couple of her business cards so I can call her. I figured you'd like one too."

"Thank you. Yes, I would." I took the proffered card and slipped it into my cash box.

"If you don't need me anymore, I'm out of here. My feet are killing me and I have some programming still to do this evening."

"Take off. I don't have too much longer to go myself. Are you bringing Shasta in the morning?"

"I think so, but if I do, I'll have to leave on time tomorrow. She can only handle so much of the stimulation here."

"She's still a puppy. You know if you want to protect her part of the time, you can put her in with Juan and Joseph. That area is much quieter than out here."

"That's a good idea. OK, I think I'll bring her. See you tomorrow."

"Have a good evening."

She was already heading for the door. Obviously she had had enough for the day. I turned back to my booth and started to take a quick inventory. I was sure that there were items that I needed to restock for tomorrow. I always enjoyed the Fiber Gathering, but this year felt like it had been weeks instead of just three days so far. I was looking forward to the closing tomorrow. I wondered how Jonathon felt about it, though. It would make his work harder when we all scattered to our various home locations. It seemed to me that we had no more answers than we did on Thursday morning.

"There she is."

I looked up to see Leslie and Jeevana heading toward the booth with their arms laden with shopping bags. The two best friends couldn't create a greater contrast if that had been their desire. Leslie was a slight bit taller than me, slim and in great shape from her running and working in the family feed store. Recently, she'd started letting her light blond hair grow out from her former pixie do, and right now it just reached the level of her shoulders in a stylish swinging cut. Jeevana's father came from India, and she took after that side of her family. She was all of five feet tall and petite in every way. Her long black hair was braided and wound up on her head. Her dark eyes reflected her laughter as they came up to the booth.

"You guys look like you've bought out the Gathering. Did you leave anything for the people coming tomorrow?"

"Oh, maybe a little," Leslie said. "We left you for last because we figured that we didn't need to buy anything here."

"What, you shop 'til you drop and you leave me out?" I tried to frown as I said it but failed.

"Not like you don't rake in our money on a regular basis," Jeevana said and laughed.

"So, did you get a fleece, Jeevana?" She had limited her fiber purchases lately because she wanted to get a raw fleece and prepare it herself.

"Two," she said. "They're kind of like potato chips. Aren't they?"

"Yep. I'm surprised you got away with just two."

"She wouldn't have if I hadn't dragged her out of there," Leslie chimed in.

"I still had one more table to look at, when she got nasty about it. You'd think she had to pay my bills."

"Nope, I just have to listen to you gripe when you've gone over budget."

"Not true, I don't gripe."

"Now, you two," I put in, "enough already. What did you get, Leslie?"

"Some silk blend roving in a lovely teal color. Want to see?"

"Sure, give me a look and feel." She pulled out her roving, and I ran it through my fingers. "This will be lovely to spin,

Leslie, and I think the staple lengths are such that you shouldn't have problems with the silk. But what is this?" I was looking at some lovely light green yarn that had come out of the bag with the roving. It appeared to be acrylic, very soft, and screamed baby-something to me.

A grin spread clear across Leslie's face and sparkles filled her eyes. "Yep, you're right. Jack and I are expecting. We're thrilled, and I wanted to start knitting right away. That's for an afghan."

"Congratulations, I'm happy for both of you. It'll be beautiful and I know that love'll be knit into every stitch."

"Mommy, we saw the baby sheeps, and Aunt Martha's alpaca. Daddy says they are cousins to camels. Did you know that, Mommy?"

A bundle of energy came running down the aisle and plowed into Leslie's legs, gathering them in a big hug. Jack was coming at a slower pace behind.

"Sounds like you and Tyler had a great time," I said to Jack.

"We did. I didn't think I'd ever get him away from the lambs. He wanted to name all of them and would've taken some home, if he could have."

"You guys are going to need to get a house with some acreage. The apartment isn't going to big enough for long, and Tyler does need a pet or two."

"You're preaching to the choir, Martha. We just need to find the right place, and that's hard. We don't want to be too far out of town and cost is a factor."

"I'll keep my ears open," I said. "I'm sure something'll come up."

Tyler had wandered over to talk to Denali, who was lying in the back of the booth, while we were talking. They'd become friends over the months since he first met her while she was recovering from surgery.

"Nali, did you know that baby sheeps are called lambs?" he asked, as he got down on the floor next to her and curled up with his head resting on her side. "I bet you did. You're smart, Nali." She just gave him a snuffle in answer, quite content to let him lie next to her.

"Looks like we have one tired boy. Guess we should take him home, big guy." Leslie directed this to Jack.

"Yep, but don't do anything sudden yet, because I want to get a picture first," Jack said as he pulled out his cell phone. "We don't see him quiet very often," he added with a grin. He got his picture and then walked over to the boy and the dog.

"Hey, pardner, are you ready to go get that cheeseburger and head home?"

"I guess so. Can Nali go with us?"

"No, she needs to stay with Aunt Martha to guard the sheep and alpaca, but we'll see her again soon. I promise."

"OK." Tyler got up and gave Nali a hug. "Bye, Nali." And then he lifted his arms. "I tired. Carry me."

"Here we go," Jack said as he reached down and gathered up his son.

"Guess we're out of here," Leslie said. "See you next Thursday if not before."

"Me too," Jeevana added. "My feet're killing me."

"Off with all of you. I only have a few more minutes and I'm out of here too."

I watched them go out the door and then turned back to the booth. Things had really slowed down as we did only have a few minutes before we closed for the day. I took the break to get my shelves tidied up and then as the closing bell rang, I put the sheets over my tables to protect things overnight.

"Come on, Nali. Let's go check on Juan and Joseph and take ourselves home."

I hooked on her leash and we walked across the arena. I went by the stalls with Catalin's lambs in them. They were still well taken care of. My guess was that Rex was taking care of that duty. I'd have to talk to Sheila about one of them. I really did want to get one if she was willing to sell it.

As I walked toward my stall, I saw something white on the door. A little concerned about my boys, I picked up my pace. As I approached closer, I saw that it was a folded piece of paper. If someone had a question, why didn't they just come ask me? But then, I wasn't always easy to find today. I picked up and unfolded the page.

"Stop meddling, bitch!" It was sloppily printed in all capital block letters. Now who? I thought of back in February and pulled out my cell phone.

"Jonathon, are you still in the arena?" I asked as he answered.

"Just getting ready to leave. What's up?"

"Want to come to the stall where I have Juan and Joseph? I have something to show you."

"Will do. Be right there."

While I waited for him, Nali and I went into the stall, and she took the opportunity to check them out. After giving both alpaca a good sniff, she lay down on the straw while I made sure they had food. I'd just gathered up the pail to get them some fresh water when Jonathon walked up.

"What's up?"

"Let me get out of here, and I'll show you. Nali, you stay where you are for a moment." I carried the pail out of the stall and closed the door behind me.

"I found this on the door to my stall," I said as I handed Jonathon the note.

He whistled softly. "Someone's warning you off. If I were you, I'd listen to him and to your friends who have been doing the same."

"But I really haven't been doing anything. All I've done is keep my eyes and ears open. I haven't even indicated to anyone other than some close friends that I doubt the accident verdict."

"Well, someone doesn't believe that. We've had one person killed and another attacked savagely. You be careful and keep a friend or one of those big dogs with you. It's important."

"I will, I promise. I always have the dogs with me when I'm home and Mark will be there this evening."

"Well, finish up what you need to do here, and I'll walk you to your van."

"OK, I'll just be a minute or two."

I picked up the pail and went to the nearby water spigot to fill it. I soon had the alpaca watered and, giving them a carrot and a quick pat, I gathered up Nali's leash and we went out, closing the stall door.

"OK, let's go," I said to Jonathon. "Did you learn anything important this afternoon?"

"Not really. It's amazing how so many people can be around and no one sees anything. And with this group it isn't a matter of not wanting to help the cops or being afraid of them, they just aren't very aware of what's happening around them and they don't see."

"Did Loreena find you?"

"She did and her information was interesting. I'll follow up on that."

As we walked down the aisle toward the door, we had to

pass the stall where Catalin was killed. I wondered again just what happened in there. There was something about the stall that bothered me, but I couldn't quite put my finger on it. It was pretty much like all the other stalls along this side of the building. They were large and roomy and built to be a comfortable place for a horse to be stabled. I glanced at it again and then concentrated on what Jonathon was saying.

"I got a call from the hospital a few minutes ago. Sheila's out of surgery and, for now, in the ICU unit."

"That's good news. She seems to be a fighter. I sure hope she makes it."

"Me too, for more reasons than one. Well, here's your van. Have a good evening. I'm sure I'll see you tomorrow."

"Thanks, Jonathon. Take care and get some rest."

He just smiled at me and headed for his car. His walk seemed a little slower this evening. The attack on Sheila was weighing on him.

Chapter 17

Falcor was at the back gate with his tail wagging when Nali and I pulled into the driveway. He greeted us with a bark as I opened the van door. I leashed Nali as I got her out of her crate and we headed to the back gate. As soon as I let her loose, she and Falcor checked each other out and then did a race around the pasture and back to me.

"Glad to have her back, are you, big guy? Let's get everyone fed and watered so I can collapse for the night."

The dogs followed me into the barn. One of the lambs was raising Cain and I went over to check it out. It was Koma, the young Jacob wether. He'd managed to get himself separated from the other lambs and couldn't figure out how to get past the equipment he'd gotten behind to rejoin them.

"Silly lamb, why'd you go into there? OK, let's get you out of here." I dug my hand into the wool on the back of his neck and guided him around the equipment and back to the others.

While I had them all together, I gave the lambs a quick check-over. All were in good shape and healthy and all had lovely fleece. Their first shearing would give me some beautiful wool to work with.

I finished feeding the livestock, topped off their water, and fed the dogs. Giving one more look out across the pasture I shut the big doors to keep the sheep and goat in for the night. The dogs could leave via their dog door whenever they chose. Secure in the knowledge that everyone was safe and happy for the evening, I returned to the house to get ready for Mark. I had just enough time for a shower if I hurried.

I was just coming out of the bedroom when I heard the dogs bark and saw his van pull into the driveway. I opened the back door for him and then went to search the refrigerator for salad to accompany the pizza.

"Hey, beautiful," Mark said as he gave the back of my neck a nuzzle. "What you looking for? I thought I brought dinner."

"Hmmm." I turned around and gave him a hug and a quick kiss. "But I thought we might have some salad to go with it. That way at least part of dinner will be healthy."

"Let's live dangerously and just have pizza and beer. I picked up an ale from Hawai`i that I wasn't familiar with, but thought that we might enjoy. It's Mehana Mauna Kea Pale Ale, and it's made on Hawai`i."

"I don't know it, but it sounds good and I love trying new food and drink. Well, if we aren't going to be healthy and need plates and utensils, let's just sit in the living room and use the coffee table. Bring the pizza and I'll bring the beer, glasses and napkins."

We gathered up everything and were soon settled on the sofa. I'd curled up in the corner with my feet under me, my favorite position for sitting. Mark was in the middle of the couch where he could reach the pizza easily, and he handed me a piece on a napkin. I took a bite while he poured our beer.

"Good. You must have bought it at Jocko's. I don't think any of the chains can make pizza like this." Jocko's was the local pizza place that had been making pizza for Black Hills residents for over fifteen years. They pretty much had the loyalty of the locals when it came to pizza for dinner. They weren't open for lunch, which gave the local chain outlet a chance to at least survive.

"I did; called ahead and it was ready for me when I got there. They really do make the best pizza in this part of the state."

"Can't argue with you there. Want to hand me my beer since you seem to be bent on waiting on me?"

"Here you are." He handed me mine and reached for his own. "Cheers," he said as he raised his glass and took a sip.

"Cheers." I sipped my beer and then sipped it again. "This is nice. I'm glad you found it. Where's it brewed again?"

"Hilo."

"I didn't know they had a brewery there. All you hear about is the Kona Brewery, but I like this a lot. I'll have to watch for it. How did the necropsy go?" I continued as I reached for another piece of pizza. I hadn't realized how hungry I was. The soup I'd had for lunch with Ellen seemed like a distant memory.

"Physically, it went just fine. Everything was pretty straightforward. Emotionally, it was harder. She was a young dog in beautiful health and obviously cared for by Sheila. Since she was with her at the Gathering, I'm guessing that she was her constant companion. It'll be hard on her."

"Were you right? Was the cause of death a blow to the head?"

"Yes. It would have knocked her out right away. Which is good because it took her a little while to die. She shouldn't have suffered though after the first blow."

"But why kill the dog?"

"My guess is that our killer used the dog to get Sheila into the tack room, and he might have only meant to silence it and hit it too hard."

"I doubt it," I said. "He'd want it to stay silenced because it would give away Sheila's location if it started barking."

"True."

"Oh and I have something else to tell you about." I filled him in on the note that I had found on the alpaca's stall at the Gathering.

"What did Jonathon say when you showed it to him?"

"That I should pay attention and follow the warning."

"I agree with Jonathon. You need to back off from all of the murder stuff."

"But I haven't even really done anything. I haven't even talked about it with anyone but close friends. I'm not out looking for clues. I don't think anyone knows that Nali found the rock except for you, Jonathon and Ellen."

"I still don't like it. Want me to stay here tonight?"

"Thanks for the offer, but no. I have the dogs. I'll be just fine."

"I'm not totally content with that, but I'll let it go for now. You stay vigilant."

"I will. Oh, Sean came by today. While we were talking, I mentioned to him that this attack would take Sheila off my suspects list, and he came up with a scenario where she could stay on it." I told him about Sean's theory.

"I guess that's possible, but I'd find it a bit of a stretch." Mark reached for my feet and started massaging them.

"Oh, you can do that forever. Standing on them all day is a killer and something they're not used to."

"Want to know what I found out from the casino?"

"Hmmm, I guess so," I said as I shut my eyes and slid a little further down into the sofa so my head was resting on the arm.

"The answer is that Kelmen is a regular at the casino where you thought you saw him, and he seems to prefer the games of skill to the games of total chance. Which may be bad luck for him because he doesn't seem to be very good at it. Conceivably, he could be over his head with gambling debts owed to someone, especially if Catalin and/or his father were keeping him on a student's short financial leash."

"So he could well have a motive for killing Catalin if he thought he were going to inherit her money. Even the insurance policy that he is getting might be a big help if he's being threatened in some way."

"I'd think so."

"So we have Rex, who was in a battle with her over property. Then we have Joseba, who had real issues with who she was and inherits all of their parents' property with her death, and we have Sheila, Kelmen and Joseba, all of whom might believe that they were going to inherit her assets. We haven't really trimmed that list down much, have we? Other than I would put Sheila to the bottom of the list, given the attack on her."

"No, we haven't. I don't think we will do it tonight, and I'm not sure you should be working on it at all."

"I know, I know. But I can roll it around in my head. Can't I?"

"You can, but I'm not sure that you'll just do that. You have a penchant for pushing just a little too hard and too far."

"One time and now I make a habit of it. Not fair." There

was just a bit of a pout in my voice this time around, but I knew that my curiosity would always get the best of me if faced with similar unanswered questions.

Mark just gave my toes a squeeze.

"So tell me something happy that happened in your life today," I said as I sat back up and reached for a third slice of pizza. I was going to regret this later, but it sure tasted good right now.

"I got to have dinner with you," he quipped.

"Besides that obvious fact," I said.

"I got to do a well puppy checkup on a litter of beautiful black lab puppies. So I received a full complement of puppy breath and puppy kisses. They're ready to go to their new homes in the next couple of weeks healthy and well socialized."

"That could help make up for a lot."

"Your turn now. What was fun in your day?"

"I got to watch Tyler curl up with his head on Nali's side and tell her that baby sheeps are called lambs, and Leslie told me that she and Jack are expecting."

"Tyler is one cute, little ball of energy. It must have taken a bit to get him to the point of collapsing with Nali."

"I think he had taken in the whole Gathering at a run with Jack in tow. I'm not sure who looked more tired."

"And great news on the advent of a baby."

"Yes, it is. Leslie had said that they wanted to start a family as soon as possible so there wouldn't be too much space between Tyler and the new baby, but I don't think she had any idea that it would happen quite this fast."

"Only takes once," Mark said with a grin. "But it's getting late, and you have one more day at the Gathering so I should be on my way. At least cleanup is easy. Want to put those last two pieces of pizza in the fridge for breakfast tomorrow?"

"How did you know that I love pizza for breakfast?"

"Just a good guess."

We gathered up the dinner stuff and moved it to the kitchen where I put the pizza on a plate for a quick warm up in the microwave in the morning. Mark put the glasses in the dishwasher, the pizza box went into the trash and the beer bottles into the recycling bin. When all was taken care of, Mark gathered me in his arms for a big hug and a slow gentle kiss.

"See you tomorrow. Have fun, but be careful. We still have a murderer out there. Don't forget we have a dinner date for tomorrow."

"I haven't, and I'll be careful," I said as I walked him out the door and onto the back porch. "I don't know a thing so I'm no danger to anyone."

"Yes, but they may not know that. Want me to shut the outside gate?"

"Please."

I watched as he got into his van and drove out of the yard. He stopped and shut the gate and then gave one beep on his horn as he drove away. I walked to the inside gate where the dogs were waiting for me.

"Come on, big guys, it's very much time for us to call it a day."

I turned and walked to the back door and inside. After checking out their territory in the front of the property, they'd follow using the dog door.

Chapter 18

Juan and Joseph hummed as Falcor and I walked toward their stall. "I guess they're glad to see us, big guy." I said to Falcor as I opened the stall. "Just one more day, fellas, and you're out of here. I'm very sure that you're more than ready for some freedom."

I picked out a few pieces of straw as I ran my hands over each of them. Although I had blown out their coats before I brought them here, they'd picked up new stuff from the floor of the stall. They still had full fleece and would be sheered as soon as the Fiber Gathering was over. I'd delayed it a little longer than usual because they were going to be on display. I already had plans for Juan's lovely cinnamon fiber. Joseph's black was still a question mark, but I was sure that I'd find some good use for it. A greater noise level made me realize that it was time to quit enjoying the company of my animals and head over to my booth. I put out fresh water and food for them, and then after giving each one a parting pat and a piece of apple, I opened the stall door. Falcor just looked up from where he was curled up on the straw.

"Want to stay with them for a bit?" His head went back down, so I took that for an affirmative answer and shut the stall door behind me as I left.

As I walked past the stall where Catalin had been killed, I realized what was bothering me. There wasn't enough blood. If her head had hit the tack box hard enough to kill her, shouldn't there be more blood? The only blood that I saw was a small amount on the corner of the tack box. There wasn't even a whole lot of blood where her head had come to rest on the straw. Scalp wounds usually bleed pretty profusely. Could she have been killed someplace else and hauled in here later after everything had settled down for the night? Had someone put the blood on the tack box to make it look like she'd hit her head on it? I mused over those questions as I went on into the main part of the arena and my booth.

"Here, you take her," Ellen said as she handed me a very frisky Shasta. "I need to get the handouts and information back up on these tables."

"Hey, pretty lady, are you being a problem?" Shasta answered me by standing up on her back legs and starting to place her front paws on me. However, she was still a little small to be able to get the paws to the top of my shoulders, so rather than having them land in a less comfortable position, I grabbed them as they came up and pulled her in for a hug.

"Whoa, Shasta, you're feeling good this morning, aren't you?" She looked up into my eyes and grinned as only a dog very pleased with itself can grin. "OK, enough. Time to get all four paws on the floor." I gave her a gentle shove and she gracefully stepped back and landed softly on her front feet.

"Do they do that often?" a voice said.

I turned to see an elderly gray-haired man who was pushing a woman of about the same age in a wheelchair. "That dog's bigger than you are." This time I could see that it was the man who was addressing me.

"Not often and not all of them," I answered. "Some only do it when invited. Some do it when they're a bit nervous because they are out of their element. So they might do it at dog shows or places like this, particularly young ones who aren't quite sure what's required of them here. Shasta fits into that last category. She's only six months old."

"That dog is only six months old. How big will it get?" This time it was the woman asking the question.

"Well, she's about two-thirds of her adult size right now. So she still has a way to go. But when she's done, she shouldn't be heavy like a St. Bernard or a Newfoundland. She should be muscular and lean and probably weigh around a hundred pounds."

"She's pretty, but why's she here? Does she herd sheep?" The woman continued with her questions. Her face was lined from being outside and in the weather and also with lots of laugh lines. Her bright blue eyes were inquisitive. I wondered what she had done in her earlier days.

"Well, actually they are used to guard sheep rather than herd them," Ellen said as she came from behind the table in the Pyr booth. "I'll relieve you of the monster girl," she added to me as she took Shasta's leash. "Why don't you come over here, and Shasta and I can tell you all about her job and how she does it."

As she and the couple moved toward the Pyr booth, I noticed that the woman's hand had reached out to stroke Shasta's fur.

Now that Shasta was with Ellen, I turned my attention to my booth. I'd brought in a couple of bins with replacement items before Falcor and I'd gone to visit the alpaca. It took me just a few minutes to get those things where they belonged. I was now ready for the Sunday crowd, and just in time, because I heard the opening bell advising everyone that it was time for sales.

I was busy helping a woman choose between two different colors of yarn when I caught sight of Jonathon out of the corner of my eye. He was heading in my direction on a pretty straight line so I figured he wanted to talk to me, but he went by me to the Pyr booth to talk to the dogs while I finished my sale. As the woman gathered up her package and headed down the row of vendors, Jonathon moved over to my booth.

"What brought you out so early on a Sunday morning?" I asked.

"I had some information for you, and I'm just restless. This case is going nowhere and all of you will pack up and go home at the end of the day. That'll make a difficult case even harder."

"That's true. Is the case now officially a murder?"

"Yes, it is. The rock that Nali found does have Catalin's blood on it and the fiber that was caught in her ring is human hair. Now the question is, whose hair?"

"I don't suppose you can just ask all of the suspects to produce a piece of their hair for testing?"

"Not without a warrant and I'd need more than our suppositions to get one of those."

"So we're back to square one."

"Yep."

"Something about the stall had been bothering me yesterday, but I couldn't put my finger on it. Then this morning, I realized what it was. There's almost no blood in the stall. Shouldn't there be more, considering the extent of her injuries?"

"Since the death had been called an accident, we might not have spent as much time as we should have checking it out. I'll go over and look at it again, but doubt that we missed anything terribly important."

I watched him walk in the direction of the stalls. There just didn't seem to be anything of consequence that Jonathon could grab onto to move forward and find Catalin's murderer.

"Can you tell me why these two skeins of yarn are so different in price?" I turned to see a dark-haired woman holding a skein of my handspun and one of a good quality commercial yarn.

"Sure. This skein is handspun. To get this skein, I had to buy the fleece or sheer it off of one of my sheep, clean that fleece, comb or card the fiber and dye it and/or blend it with other fiber, and then spin it. The second skein you're holding is an excellent quality commercially spun yarn. All of that work that I did by hand was done at some level or another by machines. Also, the fleece was purchased in large lots so the price was less."

"OK, so I understand the price difference and can see why your handspun would be more expensive, but why should I want to use it over the commercial yarn?"

"You might not want to. I personally don't use handspun to knit socks. A lot of spinners do, but I'm hard on socks and I'd rather use commercial yarn for them. I also would probably not use handspun for a large item like an afghan, especially if it were one I'd want to wash frequently."

"What I want to do is a shawl for my best friend."

"In that case, you might want the handspun. Are you doing an open lace pattern shawl or something more substantial?"

"It will be lace, but my first lace so I need it to be a fairly simple pattern."

"Then I'd recommend either a feather and fan pattern or a candlelight pattern. Both are quite easy to do, although like all lace, they do require you to pay some attention to the pattern. Here, I can show you both patterns," I said as I moved to pull out a notebook that featured different single pattern sheets. "And I actually have the candlelight pattern knit up into a scarf," I said as I pulled one of my samples down from where it was displayed and handed it to her.

"Was this knit with handspun?"

"No, it wasn't because I knew it would be used as a sample and could take a beating in the shop. I did, however, knit a shawl for me in that pattern where I used Great Pyrenees hair as part of the yarn. It is lovely and incredibly warm."

"I like the candlelight pattern, and I think I want to do it in your handspun. This will be a very special shawl. Which yarn would you recommend?"

We moved over to where I had my handspun yarn displayed. I pulled out quite a few of my skeins and checked the yardage before I handed them to her. Nothing would be worse than to have her fall in love with a skein only to learn that it didn't contain enough yarn for her pattern. I soon had five different selections for her to choose from.

"OK, first, is there a color here that you hate?"

"I'm not fond of this one," she said as she handed me a skein that was predominately yellows and greens.

"Then let's set it aside and not consider it. Now, are there a couple where you really like the colors?"

"Oh, yes. I love this one with the earth tones and the one with the blues and greens."

"Good, now we can talk about the yarn and what it contains in the way of fiber. The blue and green one is a blend of Merino and silk. It's quite soft as you can feel and the yarn'll give you very good definition of your pattern when you knit the shawl. The second one is a blend of Blue-faced Leicester and dog hair. The BFL is soft by itself and the dog hair just increases the softness of the yarn. A shawl made out of this will be quite warm because of the dog hair. It'll also get a bloom on it like you see on an angora sweater. This bloom will make your lace pattern less distinct. You'll still be able to see it, but you'll have the fuzzy edges."

"Will the one with dog hair smell like dog?"

"No," I said. "Here let me show you." I walked over to the table of the Pyr booth that separated it from me and picked up and handed her a scarf that was there for demonstration purposes. "This scarf was knit with a blend of Great Pyrenees hair and wool. To be honest, I don't remember which wool was blended in. It does have a little more Pyr hair than the skein that you're looking at, but it gives you an idea of how it feels and smells."

She ran her hands over the scarf and then wrapped it around her neck.

"Oh, this is really nice, and I see what you mean by bloom. So my shawl'll get this fuzzy soft feel to it."

"Yes, it will."

"Then I think I'll take the skein with the dog hair. I love the colors and if it feels like this, I know my friend'll love it."

"OK, now I have one more choice for you to make. I can sell you the candlelight pattern as a single pattern sheet or I can sell you a book that has this pattern and about eight others while giving you tips on knitting lace. Here, let me show you the book."

I pulled out one of my books on lace and handed it to her.

"What is the difference in price?" she asked as she leafed through the book.

"The book is sixteen ninety-five and the individual pattern is three ninety-five."

"I think I'll just take the individual pattern. The yarn was a little over my budget and I can always get the book later if I decide that I love lace."

"That's very true. I'll put a business card in with your yarn and pattern and you can always come by the shop if you have questions or if you want to get the book. I don't charge for answering quick questions from customers. That doesn't come under the heading of private knitting lesson."

"That's good to know," she said as I handed her her package. "I'll probably take you up on the offer. I hope you have a good day."

"You too," I said as she walked over to talk to the dogs at the Pyr booth.

Noticing the time, I realized that Falcor had been in with the alpaca for quite awhile. I looked at the Pyr booth and saw that Ellen had put Shasta in a crate for a rest and was not terribly busy now that other people were there with dogs. I moved over to where I could catch her attention without shouting.

"Would you watch my booth for awhile? I imagine that Falcor could use a walk."

"No problem. Take off."

Falcor must have heard me coming because he was standing at the door of the stall waiting for me.

"Time for a walk, big guy?" I said as I hooked his leash to his collar. He followed me out of the stall and waited as I made sure the door was secure. We headed out of the main doors and into the bright spring sunshine. After the rain yesterday, we were blessed with another beautiful day, and I was comfortable in just a sweatshirt jacket over my long-sleeved tee.

"You take the lead," I said and followed him without a whole lot of thought as he rambled among the various buildings, sniffing here and marking there.

As we came around the corner of the stable where Sheila was found, I saw Kelmen standing about half-way down the building. What was he doing here? He wasn't a vendor nor a shepherd. Neither his aunt nor Sheila were here so why should he be back?

"Hey, Kelmen," I said as we drew closer to him. He jumped a foot, spun around and then backed off a bit as he saw Falcor.

"You startled me. Is that dog safe? Aunt Catalin's could be pretty vicious."

"He's perfectly safe as long as I'm safe," I said. "They're usually only aggressive when something that belongs to them is threatened. You aren't planning on attacking me, are you?"

"No, ah, of course not."

"Well, then you don't have anything to worry about, do you?"

"I guess not."

"What brings you out here today?"

"I don't know. I just was all upset over Aunt Catalin and now Sheila. She was like an aunt too. After all, she'd been with Aunt Catalin forever. I can't imagine why anyone would stab her. She was great and gentle."

Stab her? Had the news said anything about how she was injured? I couldn't remember if I'd even paid attention to what the morning news had said about the incident.

"Well, I'm sure that she'll recover. She might need help on

the ranch while she's healing, though. You might want to think about helping out there."

"Helping out? Oh yah, I guess I should. Thanks. Well, I better be going."

Falcor and I watched as he turned and walked toward the parking lot. "You make him that nervous, big guy? Or was it that we saw him here at all? What was he really doing here? Well, whatever it was, we'd better get back to the booth. Ellen'll be ready to go back to big white dogs, I'm sure."

I swear these dogs do understand English. Falcor looked up at me and started walking toward the door that would lead us into the arena next to the Pyr booth. Shasta was holding forth with Ellen in my booth when we got there and totally delighted to see Falcor. He, on the other hand, didn't seem quite so enamored with the bouncy puppy, but ever the gentleman, he let her sniff him all over and bounce around him for awhile before he moved to the back of the wall and lay down.

"I gather she was done with crates," I said to Ellen.

"Yep and she was letting me know it too. Decided if the people next door were going to be able to answer any questions, I'd better bring her over here. Actually she sold two skeins of handspun with dog hair for you. Two women were commenting on how soft she was and I was able to point them to your yarn. They didn't blink at the price, just grabbed it. Shasta thinks she should get a commission."

"She does, huh? Think she'd settle for a cookie?"

Shasta answered that question because she whirled around when I said "cookie" and sat right in front of me.

"That scamp." Ellen was trying hard not to laugh as she watched her dog.

"A total charmer, she is," I said as I reached into my pocket and came up with a dog cookie for her.

Our conversation was stopped as two women came up to browse in the shop and Ellen took her pup next door to charm the visitors over there for awhile. The next hour went by quickly and I'd just finished selling a spinning wheel to be picked up the next week at the shop when my phone rang.

"Good morning."

"Martha, it's Jonathon. I've just gotten word that Sheila is conscious and I can talk to her. Would you like to join me?"

"Yes, I would, but I need to see if Ellen is willing to take over my booth once again."

Ellen had looked up when my phone rang and she nodded when I looked over her way.

"She says yes. Do you want me to meet you at the hospital?"

"Why don't you come by the police station since you have to come through town anyway? We can ride in together."

"OK, I'll need to make sure dogs are walked and settled before I leave. So will probably be between twenty and thirty minutes."

"I'll be watching for you."

"See you soon."

"Now what do I do with the dogs?" Ellen said as she and Shasta came back over to my booth,

"How about you walk Shasta and then I put both she and Falcor in with Juan and Joseph? My guess is once she is in the quieter area with the animals, she'll just fall asleep."

"Sounds like a plan to me. I think she'll just follow Falcor's example and we know he'll just curl up with the alpaca and snooze."

I watched as she and Shasta headed out the door. What would Sheila be able to tell us? Had she seen anything of her attacker? Well, we'd know pretty soon. As I was mulling over that, I looked across the arena to see Rex near the pen with Catalin's sheep. Someone had been taking good care of them and I assumed it was he. And that brought up the question again. Could he have possibly killed Catalin? Could an argument have escalated to violence? He was a big man, much taller and stronger than she. But would he have struck her with a rock? Could he have shoved her and she have hit her head on the rock? So many questions and no answers.

"Are you with us?" Ellen broke me from my reverie as she and Shasta walked up.

"Yes, just thinking about Catalin's murder. Well, if you'll give me your girl, I'll take the dogs to the stall and be on my way. I'll owe you something really big when this Gathering is over. I think you have worked my booth more than I have."

"That's OK, I'll think of some way to exact vengeance," she said with a smile. "Now take my dog and go."

I obeyed orders and gathered up both dogs on their leashes and headed for the stall with the alpaca.

"Here you go, monsters. Lie down and have a snooze. I'll get you when I get back."

I shut them in the stall and watched as Shasta first walked over and sniffed Juan and Joseph who, being used to big white dogs, just stood there, and then followed Falcor's lead and curled up on the straw to sleep. She'd be fine there and happier than in the crate at the Pyr booth.

Chapter 19

It took me about fifteen minutes to get to the police station where Jonathon was waiting for me.

"Come on and ride with me. I can get better parking."

"OK, what hospital did they take her to anyway?"

"Capitol Medical Center because they didn't figure they needed to waste any time driving across Olympia."

"Makes sense to me. She was in a very bad way when they took her out of here. How's she doing now and what did the doctors find out?"

"I was told that she's stable and expected to fully recover. She was one very lucky woman. The knife managed to miss her heart. It got one lung in two places and the other in one and tore up some muscles. Given the damage, I'm still surprised that she survived that long on the tack room floor. I promised that we wouldn't stay long and wouldn't tax her too much. They've got her on pain medication and a pump to pull the air out of her chest, and, I'm assuming, IVs for various things too."

"Thank goodness the heart was missed. I'd say that was a great deal of luck on her part. Which reminds me. Did the news stories say how she was injured?"

"I'm not sure. I didn't talk to any reporters, but I don't think the kind of injuries were kept a secret. Why?"

"Because Kelmen was wandering around the buildings today, and when I talked to him, he wondered why anyone would want to stab her. I hadn't paid attention to the stories so didn't know if they said how she'd been injured. It made me wonder if he knew something that wasn't general knowledge."

"Maybe I should talk to that young man again on general principles. He definitely has a great motive for wanting both of them dead."

"He seemed very uncomfortable while talking to me. Now that might have been caused by the presence of Falcor or maybe he had other reasons for not wanting to be seen in the area."

"Falcor could make anyone nervous if they didn't know him," Jonathon said.

"I agree. Kelmen commented that Catalin's dogs could be pretty vicious. I personally have not found Pyrs to be prone to that with people, especially people they know; but maybe Catalin preferred her dogs to have a harder edge to them."

"Rex commented that the people he sent to check on her livestock were all people who had worked with her before at some point. I think he figured that strangers might have problems with her dogs."

"That I can understand," I said. "Falcor and Denali would not take kindly to a stranger walking into their pasture when I wasn't around to say it was OK. Thank goodness I have close friends and family who could step in if needed. It could be a problem for a farmer or rancher if they didn't have help that the dogs knew."

"Boy, this traffic gets worse every day." Jonathon changed the subject as we took the exit off the freeway onto Black Lake Boulevard. "I'm so glad that I can spend most of my time in Black Hills."

"It does seem to get more and more congested."

Jonathon managed to navigate the lanes and left turns that it took to get us onto Cooper Point Drive and then Capitol Mall Drive. From there it was just a couple of minutes to the hospital parking lot. Jonathon was able to pick up a spot reserved for police so we didn't end up driving around the lot looking for a place to park.

Once inside, Jonathon explained to the receptionist who we were and whom we wanted to see, and we were given directions to the intensive care unit on the second floor.

"May I help you?" a young woman at the nurse's station asked as we got off the elevator.

"I'm Police Chief Jonathon Green from Black Hills. We're here to see Sheila Barnes."

"Oh yes, Chief Green, I was told to expect you. Sheila's in room two-fifteen. Her mother's with her. Please don't stay long and don't upset her."

"Thank you. We'll be circumspect. Come on, Martha, let's see if she can help us out at all."

We walked down the hall and Jonathon tapped gently on the door before starting to open it. However, it was opened immediately from the inside and a short, somewhat plump black woman with graying hair in a short sensible cut opened the door. There were dark circles under her eyes, and she looked like whatever sleep she'd obtained had been gotten in a chair, in the clothes that she had on at the moment.

"This is an ICU room and my daughter's not allowed any visitors," she hissed.

"Hello, Ma'am. I'm Jonathon Green, police chief from Black Hills, and this is Martha Williamson. She found Sheila. We've been told by the doctors that we can talk to her for a few minutes."

"Well, I think your business can wait. I'm not letting anyone disturb or upset my daughter right now," she said as she started to shut the door.

"It's OK, Mama," a soft voice said from inside the room. "I need to talk to them. It may help them find out who did this and who killed Catalin."

"Catalin!" Her mother almost spat out the word, "That woman has never been anything but trouble."

"Now, Mama, please let the people in the room."

Reluctantly, she opened the door and let us in.

"I'm staying just to make sure that you don't upset her."

"That's OK with me, ma'am, if it's all right with your daughter."

"It's fine, Chief Green," Sheila said in her soft voice. "What can I do for you?"

I got a good look at her for the first time. She was pale beneath her golden brown skin and obviously looked tired. There were IVs in her right arm. She had the bed in an elevated position so she could easily see us to talk to us.

"Hello, Sheila," Jonathon said. "This is Martha Williamson, who found you at the arena."

"Hi, Martha, I guess I owe you my life."

"Not me. It was Denali who found you. I probably would have just walked past the closed, locked door. It was she who insisted that we get it open."

"And who's Denali?"

"One of my two Great Pyrenees. It was her day at the show as a petting dog and demo for the Great Pyrenees booth."

"Give her my thanks then. They're terrific dogs. We, I, Catalin, oh hell, I don't know who owns them but there are eight wonderful ones on the ranch." Her eyes filled with tears and for a minute she fought for control. "And my Tessa, my border collie?"

"I'm sorry, Sheila," I said softly, "but she didn't make it. Mark Begay has her and will keep her until you let him know what you want done."

"I was afraid of that." The tears appeared again. "I just knew it in my bones. Would you tell him to cremate her and I'll pick her up later?"

"I can do that."

"Now," Jonathon said, "can you tell us anything about what happened?"

"I've kind of lost track of days, but I think it started on Friday afternoon. I was having a rather slow spell at the booth after a busy start and I decided to take Tessa out to go potty and let her run a bit. We'd gotten to the area between the main arena and the stables when she took off. I whistled, but she didn't return to me. That was very unusual for her so I followed her into the stable. I saw her go into a room off to the side and I yelled at her and called. She still didn't return, which was totally out of character. I followed her into the room and I remember saying some not nice things about her behavior as I reached to turn on the light. Just as it came on and I saw her on the floor, I was hit from behind. I woke up here where they told me that I'd been stabbed. I'm afraid that isn't much help."

"Well, it solidifies what we'd put together, but doesn't help us much with figuring out who did it."

"Did you know that you were the beneficiary of Catalin's will?" I asked.

"I knew I was at the time that she kicked me out of the house, but I figured that she'd changed it. I thought Kelmen would be beneficiary."

"No, she hadn't changed it, and we'll never know if she'd planned on it or not. Why did she kick you out?" Jonathon continued with his questions.

A shadow of pain crossed her face.

"She got into a dispute with Rex Meredith over some acreage where the two properties meet. She'd taken it into her head that it was part of her original purchase and that he'd confiscated it. I'm afraid that I told her honestly that I thought she was nuts. I couldn't fathom what put the idea into her head, but the land belonged to Rex, and it always had. She was furious with me and accused me of siding against her and even of having an affair with him behind her back. She was totally irrational on the subject and in the end, she threw me out of the house and off the ranch."

"I'm afraid that I overheard your argument with her over the lambs on Wednesday," I said. "What was that about?"

"As you know, our relationship was one that made it hard to show legal rights and ownership. Although we'd both put years of work into the ranch and both of our monies went into it and its upkeep, on paper it belonged to her. I'd never really worried about it, but when she kicked me out, my assets were there too. Although we might have worked things out in time, I was still furious when I saw my lambs at the Gathering for sale. They came from a prize ewe that I'd purchased a couple of years ago and added to our stock. I'm sure I said some pretty awful things during that argument but I never would have harmed her. Not really, I loved her. I still love her and I can't believe that she's dead." Again the ever-present tears filled her eyes.

"One last question," Jonathon said. "Do you think that Kelmen would have any reason to attack his aunt?"

She lay there silent for a moment. "I don't think so. As far as I know, he loved her dearly. He enjoyed the time on the ranch and had been coming during school vacations for a number of years. However, something had changed over the last couple of months that I was there. Nothing I could put my finger on, but something wasn't quite the same. If you ask me, her brother would be a better prospect. He hated her. In many ways, she was a better business person than he was. I think she was smarter. And then there was the matter of her sexual identity. He was beyond irrational when it came to that. If I had to give you a name of someone who'd want to harm her, I'd put my money on Joseba."

"Thank you, Sheila," Jonathon said as he handed her a business card. "If you think of anything else, please contact me. We'll let you get some rest now. Your property is being taken care of by some of Rex's staff so you don't have to worry about it. Your job is to get well now."

"Take care, Sheila," I said. "I'll give your message to Mark."

We turned to leave with Sheila's mother on our heels. She followed us out of the room and shut the door behind her.

"Find out who did this, Chief. I didn't like Catalin because I felt that she always took advantage of my daughter. But Sheila loved her, and no matter what, she didn't deserve to die, and Sheila really didn't deserve the attack on her."

"We're working on it, Mrs. Barnes. We'll figure it out as quickly as we can."

"Good," she said as she turned and went back into the room.

We walked in silence, which continued until we were in the car and back on the road again.

"Did we learn anything?" I asked.

"Really only that Sheila thinks we should be looking harder at Joseba. Pretty much her other information only confirmed what we already knew or had guessed."

"I'm guessing that Joseba'll be coming back to the Gathering this afternoon," I said. "He still thinks he should be able to pick up Catalin's animals. However, I'm assuming that you'll tell him that Rex or his designee will be returning them to the ranch until the ownership's fully determined."

"That's what I told him the last time I talked to him, but you may be correct. He's one hard-headed man. I think I'll call him again when we get back to Black Hills just to make sure that he does fully understand that and to once again get a feel for the man."

"He had motive even if you don't consider Catalin's property. He now no longer has to share the inheritance from their parents with Catalin. The means was easily obtained by anyone since it was a rock from the grounds. But did he have an opportunity? Was he the man that Loreena saw on the grounds on Wednesday? Have we missed something here?"

"Not to my knowledge, but I may come back and do some more questioning of people before you guys shut down for the day. However, I'll make that phone call first."

Chapter 20

It was just before one when I walked back into the arena.

"I understand that you went to see Sheila," Aloha said as I passed her booth. "How is she?"

"All things considered, she's doing pretty well. She'll recover fully, I'm sure." I said.

"That's good. She really seemed nice. I'm so glad that she'll be OK. Do you …"

Her question was interrupted as a woman came up to her to ask about one of her products. I just waved and went on down the line of vendors. I really didn't want to talk about Sheila much because I didn't want to mess up Jonathon's investigation. The customer gave me the chance I needed to leave without being rude. I could see Ellen at my booth about four down the line and she looked a bit frazzled. I really would owe my friend when this was over.

"Need a break?" I asked as I walked up.

"How do you manage to know just when things are going to get really busy so you can take off?"

"Just talent, I guess. Was it very bad?"

"Could have been worse. No one wanted to know about spinning wheels or looms where my knowledge is zip, but I think I probably answered or tried to answer questions on every other item in your product line. Made a few sales too."

"Thank you, my friend. Now do you want to maintain your station here while I walk dogs or do you want to walk dogs?"

"Dogs, give me dogs any day. I'll go get them gladly."

And with that she was out of my booth and heading across the arena to the stall where the dogs were snoozing the morning away.

I checked over my stock and pulled a few items from the bins under the tables to fill in some holes. Ellen'd been modest on the number of sales she'd made. Even with my gallivanting, it would be a good day if the afternoon kept up the pace.

"Can you tell me how I can use this yarn without having a terrible tangle along the way?" a woman, who'd been browsing in the shop, asked as she held up a skein of hand-dyed yarn that I carried for a friend of mine.

"There are a number of ways to do it, but they all involve getting the yarn into a ball before you begin using it. You can do like our grandmothers used to do," I continued, "and place the skein on the willing hands of a partner or if it's long enough over the back of a chair or across the arms of a chair. The idea is to keep it stretched out to its full length so that it cannot collapse on itself. Then you just start at one end and wind the yarn into a ball. The method is low tech and costs nothing.

"However, my favorite way to do it, and the way I recommend if you're going to buy a lot of yarn in skeins, is to use a swift and a ball winder. A swift is an item that will hold your skein of yarn in the stretched position. It will then rotate as you wind the ball of yarn, making that process easier. My favorite swifts are umbrella styles that are flexible in their diameter so that they work well with different size skeins. A ball winder will wind your yarn quickly into a center pull ball. Here, let me show you how they work."

I went over to the shelf where I'd placed my swifts and ball winders and pulled out two different swifts and two ball winders.

"As you can see, it opens this way," I said as I demonstrated, "and you can connect it to a table with this clamp. Once this is set up, the yarn goes from the swift to the ball winder, which is also clamped to the table, and you can wind your yarn."

"Are these expensive?"

"The two together will start at around one hundred dollars and then go up depending on how fancy you want them. The two I showed you are on a show special for forty-nine dollars each."

"Could I just buy the swift and wind my ball by hand to save money?"

"You sure could and that might be a good choice if you need to space out your purchases. Then when you have the money, you could buy the ball winder. If you take care of it, you should only need to purchase one in your lifetime."

"OK, I think I'll do that. Then I want the swift and these two skeins of yarn." She held up two beautiful skeins of my friend's yarn in warm earth tones.

"I think you'll enjoy both purchases. The yarn's dyed by a friend of mine who lives here in Western Washington. I'll put one of her cards along with mine in your package."

"Thank you. I appreciate the time you took."

"That's why we're here, and if you have any questions later, feel free to call me or stop by the shop."

I handed her package to her and she turned to go just as Ellen came up with Falcor and Shasta.

"Oh my, they're huge. What kind of dogs are they? Are they gentle?"

As if to answer her second question, Falcor walked over, sat in front of her and offered her a paw.

"Well, aren't you a smart guy," she said as she reached over to take his paw. Shasta, not one to be left out, moved in for her share of attention too.

"They're Great Pyrenees," Ellen said. "And if you're interested, you can follow me and the small monster over to our booth and I can tell you more about them. The big guy stays here."

"Thanks, I'd like to know a little more about them. Well, big guy, I'll leave you here and go talk to your friend."

She gave Falcor another pat and followed Ellen and Shasta to the Pyr booth. Falcor wandered to the back of my booth and started to lie down when his head came up and his tail began to wag. Since Ellen was right next door, I started scanning the people nearby for my brother or Mark. They're the only two other people that would cause that kind of reaction from him. I saw my brother walking down the line of vendors toward me.

"Two days in a row? Is it me, my dog or my fiber?"

He grinned. "Came with a friend, but got bored waiting at one of the booths so decided to come see if you knew anything more on the Catalin murder."

I filled him in on my morning encounter with Kelmen and the visit with Sheila.

"Sheila thinks that it might be Joseba," I said, "but it doesn't feel quite right to me. He's a nasty, banty rooster kind of guy, but in spite of his money motive, I can't quite settle on him."

"I wonder if he has any history of violence," Sean mused. "He has an explosive temper and I can see him doing something in a fit of anger. But then, why Sheila, other than to get the ranch?"

"For my money, in spite of all his protestations that he loved his aunt and Sheila, I think that it could well be Kelmen. His schoolmates say that his studies have slipped lately. One commented that he'd changed over the last few months. And Mark found out that he's been gambling heavily at Sky Mountain. Might be that someone is putting a lot of pressure on him for payment of a debt. He might be gambling somewhere other than the casinos."

"Could be. I wonder…"

"There you are. I thought I'd find you here." Jeevana interrupted Sean as she walked up.

I looked from one to the other. "Looks like you two've been keeping secrets," I accused.

"Well, at first we just hadn't run into you to tell you, and then it kind of became a challenge to see how long we could keep the gossip mill from taking off," Sean offered.

"I haven't even told Leslie," Jeevana added. Leslie was Jeevana's best friend. "But we decided we wanted to come here today, or I decided that we wanted to come here. Sean's being a good sport. So we figured that it would be out to the world after this afternoon."

"So how long have you been keeping this secret?"

"Since the party for Jack and Leslie in late February. We got to talking there and one thing led to another," Sean said. "Must admit that I find this little gal to be pretty special."

Jeevana gave him a playful punch in the ribs and grinned up at him. Small and petite, she looked even smaller next to my six-foot-plus brother.

"Well, I must admit that I think it's great news. You're both pretty special to me, as you know. Enjoy the ride and don't rush things."

"Don't worry," Jeevana said. "We're taking this one slow and easy. I know that Sean got burned once before, and I'm in no hurry to make a big commitment."

My brother was still recovering from a rather nasty divorce that happened at the end of last year.

"Well, I have two more booths to hit to see if they've marked anything down so they can sell it rather than take it home. Want to come with me or stay here?" Jeevana asked Sean.

"Found out what I wanted to know here so guess I'll keep you company. Call me if you learn anything else, Sis."

"Will do. You two enjoy the rest of your afternoon." I watched as they walked away hand in hand. I couldn't think of anyone that I'd rather have for a sister-in-law if things worked out that way.

"Well, that was a pleasant surprise," Ellen said and then grinned. Like me, she was very fond of Jeevana.

"I know, and I can't believe that they managed to keep it a secret in our town for a couple of months."

"Obviously the Black Hills underground is slipping."

"So how long are you here for today? I asked her.

"I've about thirty more minutes on my official shift, but I'll probably stay around to the end so that I can help tear down the booth. A couple of more hours won't hurt and I know that the late shift will need help."

"I'll be very glad for it to be over. This Gathering was very much not what I'd anticipated when I drove in here on Wednesday afternoon to set up. Although, thanks to you, I'll have done fairly well in the sales department. I don't know what I would've done without you."

"Don't worry, I'm about to take out my pay in spinning lessons. I fiddled with a couple of the spinning wheels while in your booth and I'm going to buy one when everything gets back to the shop and you can show me the ins and outs of all the different brands."

"Spinning lessons! I think you've earned a considerable discount on the price of the wheel."

"Well, we can argue over that later. Just be warned that you're going to have to spend some time with me."

"And I don't know if I can handle doing that or not; I'll have to think about it."

She turned to answer a question from someone at the Pyr booth, and I turned my attention to my shelves wondering, if there were some things that I could start packing up. It was always a conundrum at the end of a show. You didn't want your shelves to start looking bare, but it would be nice to get some of the things put away so that you could break down quickly when the time came.

While looking the shelves over, my mind niggled on a problem that had been at the back of it all day. Something just didn't feel right about the area where I met up with Kelmen that morning. I couldn't bring it into focus, but there was something wrong.

"Can you tell me which of these spindles might work best for a beginner?"

I looked up to see a dark-haired, dark-eyed girl probably in her late teens holding two of the spindles that I had on display.

"There's never one best spindle, but let's talk about the differences between some of them. Both of the spindles that you're holding are top whorl spindles. I'll admit that they're my favorites, but many people prefer the bottom whorl spindles, like these." I pulled a bottom whorl from my shelf. "There're some technical differences in how they spin, but the bottom line is really which one you like best. Both'll do a good job for you."

"I like the look and feel of the top whorls," she said. "Is there any reason why I can't learn on one of them?"

"None at all. You've decided on a top whorl. Now let's look at other things that might make a difference in your decision. The first is weight. For a beginner, I recommend a spindle between one ounce and two ounces. This gives you a mid-range that lets you spin many different types of yarn. Both of the spindles you showed me fall into that weight range. Another thing to consider is cost. There's about twenty-five dollar's difference between the cost of the two spindles."

"Why so much?"

"The less expensive one's an Ashford spindle. It's made of silver beech, which is a rather common wood and it's made by machine. It's a good, serviceable and solid spindle made by a very reputable company. The other spindle is handmade in koa, which is a rare wood, by a woodturner in Hawai`i. So with the second one you're paying for a rare wood and the hand craftsmanship."

"Can I learn to spin just as well on one as the other?"

"Yes, you can, and unless you're just certain that you'll love spinning and want to do it for some time, I'd recommend that you choose the less expensive spindle. If you come to love spinning on a spindle, you'll find that you can never have too many of them and you can purchase the more expensive spindles as your interest increases and your money allows."

"Can I learn to spin from a book?"

"You can and I have a couple of excellent books for beginners. It's also possible to learn from YouTube. There are many tutorials out there. Or if you live close to Black Hills, you can come by my shop and I'll be glad to throw in a couple of lessons as part of the purchase of the spindle."

"I live in Elma, and I like that third option. May I call you next week and make an appointment?"

"Of course, I'll put a business card in with your purchase so you'll have all of my contact information."

"OK, then I'll take the Ashford spindle. I guess I'll need something to spin too."

"It usually helps. Let's find you some relatively inexpensive roving to start out with. This Romney would be good. It's an easy staple length to learn on and the fiber is quite forgiving. I have it in a number of colors. Which would you prefer?"

"Oh, I like that sort of heathery gray."

"That's the natural color of the sheep's fleece, and I agree, it's nice fiber. These packages have five ounces in them, which should get you started quite nicely, and I'll take a dollar off the price since you're buying it with a spindle."

"That should do me then. I'll take these and call you next week to make an appointment to come by."

"That sounds good. I'll look forward to your call."

I wrapped up her spindle and fiber and put my card in with it. As I handed it to her I saw her gaze go over to the Pyr booth.

"Beautiful dogs."

"They are. Why don't you go over and say hi? That's what they're here for."

"I'll do that," she said as she took her package and walked over to the Pyr booth.

She had just walked off when a woman I'd met at earlier gatherings walked up to my booth.

"Hi, Martha, I think you're going to be glad to see me today," she said.

I looked at the woman in front of me. There was nothing outstanding about her. Her hair was a dishwater blond, her eyes were an unremarkable hazel and her features, though not unpleasant, had nothing about them that would cause you to give her a second glance in a crowd. Even her height and build were an average five-three or so and just slightly overweight. But I knew that underneath all this ordinariness was the heart and soul of an artist and a very quick wit.

"I'm always glad to see you, Georgia," I said. "What took you so long to get here this year?"

"We've been up in Canada for a show where Jeremy had some pieces entered and we just got back late last night. I slept in this morning so here I am, sort of when the last dog dies, but here."

I laughed. "Don't let Falcor hear you talking about dogs dying. You might worry him. I'm really glad you made it, though. It has been ages since we've gotten together. How did Jeremy do with his pieces?"

Jeremy was Georgia's husband and pretty well known for his sculpture in the Northwest.

"He did well. He had six pieces entered and sold four. The gallery wants to keep the other two because they think they can sell them quickly. So it paid for our vacation in Victoria and quite a bit more. Well worth the trip and hassle of getting them up there. But that's not why I'm here. I'm ready to move up from my rigid heddle loom and I wondered what you had in stock and what you would recommend. My space is somewhat limited so a loom that could be folded when not in use might be nice."

"You are in luck because I have both of the folding looms that I carry in stock right now. Actually I have three, but for you, I'd recommend the larger of the Schacht Wolf looms. So I have an eight-shaft Leclerc or the eight-shaft Schacht Mighty Wolf. My personal loom is the Schacht and I've been very happy with its performance. What did you have in mind to weave that causes you to want to upgrade?"

"I've become fascinated with double weave. While in Victoria, I found a book by Jennifer Moore on it and I'm hot to try my hand at it."

"I love Jennifer's work. I have her book and I also have her DVDs in stock at the shop if you want them. Either of the looms I carry would work great to work your way through her book."

"Oh, great! I'll be there Tuesday morning, bright and shining. I can't wait to get started."

"Well, bring your large van without any back seats when you come. The looms are set up, but they will fit in your van when folded. Both have warps on them, so you can play with them a bit. Actually if you come around ten-thirty and bring Jeremy for some muscle power, we can also have lunch after you get done shopping. I'd love to catch up with both of you."

"That sounds perfect, and Jeremy has something for you so I know that he'd love to come with me. We'll be there. If anything does happen to change our plans, I'll call you."

She then noticed that Falcor had come up to sit next to me and in front of her.

"Hello, Falcor. You are ever the gentleman waiting for people to take notice. How are you today, big boy?" She then crouched down and gave him a good scratch on the chest and around the ears. "Where's your partner in crime, fella?"

"She's at home taking care of patrol duty," I said. "She's pretty much back to normal after her surgery and so I'm comfortable letting her work during the day by herself."

"I'm so glad to hear that. She gave us a good scare. Well, if I'm going to get any other shopping done at all, I need to check out the other vendors."

"Have fun, there's a lot of tempting stuff down this aisle."

"My bank account is already suffering from this stop, but I'll probably find something else that I just can't live without out. See you Tuesday."

"Looking forward to it."

She gave Falcor a last pat and waved as she moved to the booth next to me. I watched as she gave Ginger Phillips's rugs a cursory glance and then moved further down the row of vendors. That sale would really push my sales for the Gathering over the top. Although I would have made this particular sale without the Gathering. Still, nice to have it added to the financial return for this month.

The rest of the afternoon went by quickly and I was surprised when I heard the warning bell. The Gathering would be closing in fifteen minutes. With that warning, I felt quite comfortable starting to remove items from my shelves and place them into bins to take home. I started with the books and patterns and shifted them into a bin.

I then had two customers come up, breathless, who wanted

to get some of my handspun yarn. They'd waited until the last minute to see if they'd still have the money for it. Just as I finished the sale, the final bell to end the Gathering rang. Ellen and I did a high-five over the low shelves that divided my booth from the Pyr booth. Now I just had to get all of this stuff ready to haul away.

Chapter 21

"N eed help?" Ellen asked as she came over. The Pyr booth was down and the equipment had been hauled away by the member who stored it for the club. "I just have two boxes of Pyr information to haul out to my truck and I'm ready to go."

I'd emptied my shelves and all of my products plus my tablecloths were stored in my bins.

"If you could just help me fold up these portable shelves and collapse the tables, I'll be pretty much ready to start loading."

"Can do."

It just took Ellen and me a few minutes to get the rest of my equipment down and ready to go to my van.

"OK, I'm going to take Falcor out to the van and pick up my dolly. Are you ready to walk out?"

"I am."

I leashed Falcor and she picked up the boxes that she need-ed to carry. She'd taken Shasta out right before she offered to help me. We made our way down the line of vendors, who were in different stages of shutting down. Many of them wanted to give Falcor one more pet before he left, and we said our good-byes and see-you-next-years.

Soon we were at Ellen's truck. Shasta gave one little bark from her crate to say that she wasn't happy about being left there even for a short period of time.

"Hush, noisy face," Ellen said. "We're going home now and you aren't hurting."

She put her boxes into the back of her truck, turned and gave me a hug.

"Talk to you tomorrow when all has settled down."

"Will do," I answered. "I think Mark and I are having din-ner tonight, but haven't touched base with him today so don't know if it's still on."

"Well, give him a hug for me and have a great evening."

She climbed into her truck and I walked on to where my van was parked closer to the stables behind the arena.

"In you go, big guy," I said as I opened Falcor's crate. "I'll leave the van door open for you while I go back and forth. You keep an eye on things."

I took my dolly from the storage area in the horse trailer that was attached to the van so that I could haul Juan and Jo-seph home and headed back to the arena. It didn't take me long and I had everything put away. Now all I had to do was get my two alpaca and their gear and I could head for home. I'd call Mark just before I left here to see if our date was still on.

"OK, Falcor, I'll be back in just a bit with the two fuzzy ones. The door's still open for you. Keep watch."

I started back to the arena, but decided to go past the area where I'd seen Kelmen that morning. Something was still bothering me. As I got closer to where we'd stood to talk, I could see something from this angle that I didn't see when I was right on top of it. There was an area that seemed to have additional sand on it. The space between the buildings was a mix of gravel, grass clumps, low weeds and ground cover with some sand or fine gravel. But in one area there seemed to be quite a bit of sand. Some of it was on top of the surface and some seemed worked into the grass and weeds.

I walked over to it and looked down. Had the sand been added? I then remembered that there was a pile of sand in back of the buildings that had a shovel stuck in it. Had the sand come from there? If so, why? I squatted down to get a better look at it, and just as I started to sweep some of the sand away, I felt a hand on my shoulder.

Looking up I saw Kelmen and his left hand held a hunting knife with a blade nasty enough to do serious damage.

"Come with me."

I stayed squatting where I was for a moment. My mind went quickly over my options. I didn't come up with any good ones, and Falcor was locked in his crate. He'd be no help and I didn't I want him near that knife anyway.

"I said, come with me." He was totally cool and calm and there was ice in his voice. Nothing here spoke of the nervous young man that I'd talked to that morning.

"OK, I'm getting up," I said as I rose to my feet.

"This way," Kelmen indicated as he steered me toward the stable where we'd found Sheila.

"Do you think you can do it twice, Kelmen? Why Sheila? What had she done to you?"

"Now, isn't that a stupid question. She inherited the ranch. My stupid aunt left her ranch to that black bitch. It was supposed to come to me. I'm family. She isn't."

"If you think family should get it, why not your father?"

"Him. Aunt Catalin couldn't stand him. There was no chance she'd leave it to him. But to me, that was where it was supposed to go. She'd no children. I was her closest kin so it should've been mine."

"But I believe that Catalin considered Sheila family. They'd been together for over twenty years."

"Didn't keep her from throwing the black bitch out though, did it? So why wasn't the ranch left to me? I'm sure that's what she really wanted."

"I think she would've changed her will if that'd been her desire. No, Kelmen, I'm sure that your aunt wanted the ranch to go to Sheila."

As I said that, we reached the door to the stable and Kelmen gave me a shove to get me inside. Just as I entered the building, I heard Falcor start to bark. Something'd set him off. Whatever it was, I hoped that he kept on barking. It might alert someone to problems. But Kelmen also heard him and obviously he wasn't happy. He looked back over his shoulder quickly and then scanned the stable. His gaze settled on the set of stairs at the end of the building that led to the loft area above. I could see the railing for the loft, but not much of the loft itself from where we were standing.

"That way." He gave me a shove toward the stairs.

"But why kill Catalin in the first place? Wasn't she already paying for your school and weren't you going to get a share of the ranch and become part of the management as soon as you left school? Why were you in such a hurry to get an inheritance that you weren't even totally sure was yours?"

"Stupid aunt. She said she loved me, said that I was a son to her. But when I needed some money, she wouldn't lend it to me. Wanted to know why I wanted it. Said that she was already paying my school and living expenses and giving me a large amount for anything else. Why should I need more money? Tried to explain to her that sometimes a guy just does. You'd have thought that ten thousand dollars was a lot of money. Hell, I knew how much the stupid woman was worth. That was a drop in the bucket, plus she was set to inherit a bunch of money from my grandparents. She could write a check for that amount without even blinking."

"Ten thousand sounds like a lot of money to me. Why would you need that much money when all your expenses plus were paid?"

"You sound just like her. How can you women be so dumb? Sometimes a man just needs money, that's all."

We'd reached the bottom of the steps and I paused.

"Keep moving."

As I started to climb, I realized that Falcor had gone silent. There could only be one reason for him to do that. Someone had let him loose or was with him that he trusted. I hoped that someone was smart enough to trust Falcor. I got to the top of the steps and looked across the loft. It was a dead end with the bales of hay that Nali had investigated earlier at the other end. The roof of the building slanted down making the side of the loft quite shallow, maybe two bales of straw or hay high. The edge by the rail, which was still not to the center of the building had maybe seven feet of clearance above it. The flooring was just rough particleboard. In spite of it having steps leading to it, it was obviously just meant for storage. However, the railing offered some safety for anyone working up here, and I supposed it was required because it was a public building.

"Now what, Kelmen? Are you going to kill me too? You'll have to do it to my face with me watching you. You don't have the drop on me like you did with your Aunt Catalin and Sheila. Do you have the guts to kill someone while you look at them? And then what will you do? Do you think you can really get away with this for long? Sheila's alive and you still don't inherit."

As I talked, I moved in the direction of the railing. I wanted to be able to see the floor of the stable if someone came in. I also hoped to maneuver Kelmen so his back was to the railing so he wasn't as apt to see down there.

"Stupid woman. How could she live so long? You didn't find her until the next day and she was alive. How could she still be alive? You women are ganging up to make my life hard. You simply don't understand that a man has things he must do and that a man should always make the decisions."

He was beginning to make even less sense as he continued to talk. How could a young man who spent most of his time with an aunt and her partner, get such a warped idea of women and their role? Was his father that much of a misogynist? Or had Kelmen's need for money totally twisted him?

We were getting close to the railing area now. I turned my body slightly so that Kelmen had to put his back to the railing in order to continue to face me. I still didn't know what I was going to do and I was running out of topics to keep him talking, but keeping him talking was crucial.

"So, did you kill your Aunt Catalin where you just found me? Is that why the sand's on the ground? Was her blood all over there? I'm surprised that one of the dogs who spent time there didn't dig it up. Dogs can smell old blood, you know?"

"Stupid animals were another of Aunt Catalin's weirdo ideas. She really thought they were intelligent. She thought they could understand her. She thought she was talking to them. I doubt that an animal could even find you right now. They're dumb."

"She seemed to have a way with them," I said. "I watched her with her sheep and my friend's dog. She had an understanding of them."

"That's why it was so easy to kill her. I just told her that there was a lamb loose on the grounds and we needed to go get it. Of course, she wanted to know why I didn't get it, and I had to say that I couldn't. That brought some words from her that I got even for when I hit her. She went out to look for it, and I hit her. Hit her and hit her again and then I kicked her. I needed to make sure that the llama was blamed. And he was and would still have been if you hadn't gotten nosey. Couldn't keep yourself out of it, could you?"

"And what would you've done if she'd turned to look at you at just that moment? Hit her anyway? Or would you've been too cowardly to do it?" Just then, out of the corner of my eye, I spotted Mark and Falcor coming in the door. It wouldn't take Falcor long to find me and I didn't want him in a fight with Kelmen. He'd lose when up against a knife. I was going to have to do something and do it fast.

"Mark!" I yelled.

Kelmen glanced back to look over the rail and that gave me my chance. I rushed toward him just as he swung back to look at me,but my shoulder collided with his with as much force as I could put into it. His left arm crashed against the railing edge and the knife went sailing. I brought my knee up, got him in the groin, and we both went down to the floor. I could hear

Mark and Falcor on the steps. I continued to struggle to sub-due Kelmen, but he'd a wiry strength about him in spite of his small size. Just as I heard Falcor hit the top of the steps, Kelmen made a swift move and before I knew it he was on top of me with his fist drawn back.

"No, you don't." I heard Mark as he grabbed Kelmen and yanked him off of me. Taller and used to physical activity, Mark rammed Kelmen against the floor and soon had his hands be-hind him. Falcor, for his part, was at Kelmen's head growling and making it clear that he could and would attack if necessary. I pulled my belt off and handed it to Mark to bind Kelmen's hands. Then I grabbed Mark's cell phone out of his pocket.

"911—How may I help you?"

"This is Martha Williamson and I'm at Black Hills Rid-ing Academy. I need Chief Green right away. We have Catalin Ezkarra's killer. We're in the loft of the building where Sheila Barnes was found."

"Hold on, please."

I stood there waiting and wondering if I should have just called Black Hills Police directly.

"Chief Green is in that area and will be with you shortly. Are you in any danger?"

"No, I'm not. He is under control and being guarded."

I heard Jonathon's siren and then a second one in the dis-tance, then closer and then they stopped.

"I believe he's arrived. Thank you for your help."

"That's why we're here."

I hung up as Jonathon came through the door with Walter Jackson right behind and Blackie beside him.

"Walter, could Blackie stay down there? I think Falcor might take umbrage," I yelled over the railing. Pyrenees are not known for their tolerance of other dogs and Falcor was on high alert at the moment.

"Sure thing, Martha. Blackie, down and stay." The Doberman gave him a quizzical look that said "Are you crazy?" But he obeyed and went into the down stay.

"Kelmen. Why am I not surprised?" Jonathon said as he got to the top of the stairs.

"Stupid women. They're all bitches and you guys're all suckers because you let them run the show. World is all fucked up."

"I guess it is, young man." Jonathon said as he removed my belt, handcuffed him and handed me my belt. "Now you have the right to remain silent …" he continued with the Miranda rights.

As soon as Mark handed Kelmen over to Jonathon, he gathered me into his arms. As I started to shake, I realized just how close I'd come to really dying this time. Thank goodness for my beloved dog and for Mark.

"Hey, it's all right. It's all over now and we've no one to patch up this time."

I just nodded and moved further into his arms. It felt so good. Then I felt a nose come in next to me and a nudge.

"You did great, big guy. I don't know how you knew something was wrong, but you did. Thank you."

I knelt down, took his big head into a hug and buried my face in his fur. These magnificent dogs. I couldn't imagine living without them.

"Here, Walter, you and Blackie take him back to the station. I'll be there shortly, but I need to talk to Martha and Mark first." Jonathon had finished with Kelmen.

"Come with me, Kelmen," Walter, always the gentleman, said. "We've a ride to take, and don't get any ideas because I have an excellent partner downstairs."

"Another one of those dumb animal people. You're all nuts."

"Probably," Walter laughed, "but we aren't heading for jail. Now come along."

He took Kelmen down the stairs and as soon as he was at the bottom, he signaled Blackie. The Doberman was at his side in an instant and flanked Kelmen as the two of them walked him out to the waiting police car.

Jonathon turned to Mark and me. "OK, Martha, why don't you tell me how you managed to get yourself into danger this time?"

I told him just what had happened from the time I started back to the arena until Mark and Falcor rescued me.

"And you, Mark. Why were you here?"

"I promised Rex that I'd come check over Catalin and Sheila's animals one last time before he moved them back to the ranch. He didn't want to be accused of taking any kind of problem to the other ranch animals. He took it upon himself to help out with her animals, but he doesn't have any real authority to do it. He was protecting himself and wanted to make sure that all was as it should be. When I finished with that, I went looking for Martha.

"That's when I heard Falcor barking in the van. That's not normal for him nor was it an 'I'm all alone here' bark. I went over to the van where Falcor was doing everything he could think of to get out of his crate and barking like mad. I decided to trust him; and against all the rules, I let him loose without his leash. He made a beeline for the stable and I was hard pressed to keep up with him. When we came in the door, Martha yelled and you know the rest of the story."

"Well, sounds to me like the big guy has earned himself a steak once again. You're very lucky, Martha. Kelmen could have easily killed you."

"Yes, I know it. And this time, I wasn't even looking for trouble."

"Well, it found you. I'm just glad that Falcor and Mark were close by. I'd have hated to have found you like we found Sheila."

"Speaking of Sheila, any further updates on how she's doing?" I asked.

"She's improving more rapidly than the doctors expected. When I talked to her ever-watchful mother late this afternoon, I learned that they were thinking of discharging her early next week. Of course, there are arguments between mother and daughter over where she should go when discharged. Her mother wants her to go home with her. Sheila wants to get back to the ranch with her animals. Any bets on who wins that one?"

"Not from me. They're both very strong women. I guess I hope Sheila wins even if it means her mother spends some time with her. She's been away from there too long as it is. However, any chance that Joseba could get some kind of injunction to keep her out of the ranch while he fights the will?"

"I'm not an attorney, but I talked to David about it and he doesn't think so. He says that the will is drawn up quite tightly and that he and Catalin were very careful to take that possibility into consideration. He thinks that Sheila can move back in even before anything is probated on the grounds that the animals need care. At least he'll argue that if Joseba does try to block her."

"That's good. I'm glad that she has David in her corner."

"Well, I need to get to the station and talk to Kelmen. I'll need the two of you to come in tomorrow and give me an official statement that you can sign."

Mark and I agreed to do that and watched as he went down the stairs and out of the building. Then Mark gathered me in his arms again and reached down and kissed me lightly.

"Let's get your animals and take you home."

"I'm for that. Come on, Falcor," I said.

We started down the stairs with my hand on Falcor's collar. Although I was pretty sure that he would stay close right now, you never knew. I didn't want to be chasing a loose Pyr tonight.

It did not take us long to halter up Juan and Joseph and get them and Falcor loaded in the trailer and van respectfully. As Mark and I headed back to the arena to get the last of my equipment from the stall where the alpaca had stayed, I saw Rex running across the parking lot toward us, his limp hardly noticeable as he covered ground quickly.

"What is this I hear about you and Kelmen?" he asked, panting a bit from the exertion of his run. "I left right after you and I looked at the animals, Mark, and was gone for a short time running errands. I get back to hear that Jonathon was here and that Kelmen was taken away in a police car."

"Easy, Rex, slow down," I said and then filled him in.

"Kelmen, I would have never guessed. He seemed so devoted to her when I saw them together at the ranch."

"I'm not sure Kelmen has ever been devoted to anyone," I said, "and he especially doesn't seem to like women. He was able to mask it to get what he wanted. However, when she told him no, his true colors came out."

"Well, I'm glad it's over. I'm also very glad that it really didn't seem to have an effect on the Gathering. I'm hearing vendors say that they had an especially good year."

"I haven't tallied mine up, but I think I did pretty well. Especially since I ended up leaving a lot of the work to Ellen."

"I'm about ready to close this building down. You got all your stuff out of it?"

"We're going back for the last load now. Are we the last ones?"

"No, I have two others who're slow, but I'm about to hurry them along. I want to get home. I haven't been there since Wednesday morning."

"Well, then we will make quick work of getting my stuff out. Thanks for a great Gathering, Rex. I hope you have a lovely and restful evening."

He started toward the main doors of the arena and we moved toward the side door. As we walked by it, I looked once again at the spot where Kelmen had killed his aunt. It seemed like such a waste. But then, murder usually is.

Mark and I gathered up the rest of my equipment and headed back out via the main arena doors. I could see Aloha loading the last of her stuff into her van. I waved.

"It was great meeting you, Aloha. I hope we see each other again before the next Gathering."

"I'm sure we will. I'll give you a call"

I then turned and loaded my armful into the storage area of the trailer and closed the doors. Mark was standing next to the trailer talking softly to the alpaca."

"Still want to go out for dinner?" he asked.

I'd completely forgotten that we were supposed to celebrate the closure of the Gathering by eating out tonight.

"I don't think so. I'm beat."

"OK, how about this: I'll follow you home and help you unload. Then you can go in and get a shower and into something comfortable. I'll go get dinner from someplace and bring it back with me. We can eat at your house and have a very quiet evening."

"That's fine, but you don't have to follow me home. I only have to unload the animals tonight. Everything else can wait and will wait. I don't want to deal with it this evening. So why don't you go home and get that shower too and then pick something up and come by in about an hour and a half? That should give me plenty of time."

"I can do that."

With that, he gathered me up for one more protective kiss and opened the van door for me to climb in.

"Drive safely, I'll see you soon."

Chapter 22

I started the van and drove away. Soon I was turning into my driveway and could hear Denali welcoming us home with her lovely bark. I stopped just inside the gate and closed it so that I could open the gate to the back part of the property. I wanted to take no chances on loose animals tonight. I was way too tired. Soon I had Juan and Joseph in their field and Denali was giving them a good inspection to make sure everything was OK. Falcor still didn't want to get very far from me, but I could see he wanted to check out his property.

"Go, big guy, it's safe here at home." He gave me one more look and then raced across his field to make sure things were as they should be.

I moved into the barn and pulled down feed for the animals. I love working with my animals and the pungent smells of my barn, but tonight it was especially wonderful to be here when I realized how close I'd come to never being here again.

I whistled and the alpaca and goat who hadn't come in when I got home came at a leisurely pace into the barn. I shut them into their respective areas and put out the dog food. I pulled shut the large barn doors and left the dogs to eat their dinner. I closed the inside gate and walked across the yard to open the outer one. The temperature was dropping and it was going to be in the 30s tonight even if it was May.

Back in the house, I made sure that I had a white wine in the refrigerator along with some local beer and then headed for the shower. As I stood under the hot, running water, it really hit me as to how close I'd come to death myself. Without realizing it at first, tears began to run down my cheeks. Tears of relief and gratitude that my big white guy had been there for me and that Mark had listened to him. I was so grateful and so lucky. I just stood there for a bit and soaked in the pleasure and relief. Finally I decided that it was time to get out and I finished washing my hair and shut off the water.

I toweled down and toweled dry my hair. Deciding against taking the time to dry it, I just braided it into a long single braid that reached halfway down my back. Mark liked it loose, but not tonight. I pulled on some sweats and figured I was dressed for the evening. This was a take-care-of-me night and not a get-beautiful-for-my-guy night.

I had just entered the kitchen when I heard the wheels of Mark's van and the dogs' greeting. I watched from the back porch as he walked back and shut the outside gate and then opened the inside one. Evidently he thought the dogs would want to be with us. He was right, Falcor came to the back porch at a run. He didn't even stop to say hi to Mark. Denali did, though; she always had time for her very special Mark.

"Hey, big guy," I said to Falcor as he shoved up next to me.

"Still checking on me are you? Everything's fine, and we're going to have a nice quiet evening at home. And what's for dinner?" I asked, turning to Mark as he came up the steps laden with sacks.

"I stopped at Black Hills Cafe and told Sally that I needed very special comfort food for you. We have her marvelous mac and cheese, fresh crusty bread right out of the oven, a beautiful green salad with Sally's special house dressing, and malasadas for dessert. And I stopped at the grocery store and got some premium vanilla ice cream to go on top of those malasadas."

Malasadas are the Portuguese donuts that are so well loved in Hawai`i, and something I had no trouble getting addicted to while I lived there. Sally learned to make them while on vacation one year and brought them back to Black Hills. They're a hit here too.

"Sounds yummy. Sally picked some of my favorite things from her menu. Inside with you and let's eat. But," I added as we walked in the door, "I need to call Ellen. I really don't want her to hear about this afternoon from anyone before she hears it from me."

"I agree. Call her and I'll find us a glass of wine. Red or white?"

"Well, I suppose that traditionally it would be white, but I think I want red tonight. Check out the pantry. I think you can find something nice that is Washington or Oregon."

I turned and picked up the phone.

"Ellen," I said after she answered. "I need to let you know what happened after you left." That being said, I filled her in on what had happened. It took me awhile to convince her that I was just fine, that Mark was with me, and that I really didn't need her company this evening.

As I hung up, Mark handed me a glass of wine with one hand and pulled me into him with the other.

"That was way too close a call this afternoon."

"I know, but thanks to you and Falcor, I'm fine," I said and kissed him on the cheek. "Now let's get a fire going and enjoy it with our wine and then do justice to Sally's wonderful food."

Mark started the fire while I turned on some music and then rummaged through the refrigerator for some cheese and put it on a plate along with some crackers.

"This should go nicely with our wine," I said as I placed it on the coffee table and curled up on the couch next to Mark.

He reached for a piece of cheese and bit into it. "Hmmm, didn't realize how hungry I was."

"Nor how tired," I added as I snuggled up next to him and took a sip of my wine. "It won't be a late night for me, I can tell you that."

"Nor for me, especially since I have surgery scheduled early tomorrow."

"Oh, what?"

"Just a spay for one girl, and if the pups don't come tonight, a possible C-section for another. Nothing dramatic or serious, but it is scheduled for eight o'clock and I have to be alert even for routine surgeries."

I didn't feel any need to answer that, but just cuddled up against Mark, sipped my wine and listened to IZ sing "Over the Rainbow." It was good and comfortable to just be home.

"Think we should have some of Sally's food or you're going to fall asleep on me." Mark's words caught me drifting off.

"You're right. You bring the containers from Sally's to the table and I'll get out some dishes and utensils for us."

Just as we were sitting down, my phone rang.

"I'm surprised that it's taken this long," I said as I answered it and carried it to the table.

"So I take off and you get into trouble as soon as I leave."

"Hello, little brother. I see you've been talking to Walter or Jonathon or both."

"Walter and I had made a previous date for pizza and a beer and to catch up with each other. He was about half an hour late getting to Jocko's and you were his excuse. Glad Mark was handy, but you really need to keep your nose out of such things."

"I know, I know, but I really didn't do much to get into today's mess."

"Need me to come by tonight?"

"Nope, Mark's here but as soon as we finish dinner, I'm chasing him home too. What I really need is some sleep and I'll have no trouble getting it. The big guys will be here to watch over me. Falcor will hardly let me out of his sight."

"OK, but call if you need me. Tomorrow's your day off so take it easy."

"I plan to. I just have to unload the stuff from the Gathering and get my shop back in order. And I don't need to do that to anyone's timetable but my own."

"All right, sleep tight then. Love ya."

"Love you too," I said as I hung up. "That was Sean, in case it wasn't obvious."

"Guessed that. Now eat your dinner before it gets cold. The cheese is a great addition to the bread, by the way. Not that we need more cheese, but…"

"You can't have too much cheese," I finished for him.

I ate a couple of mouthfuls in silence. It really was wonderful and the bread was heavenly. Sally's place was by far the best place in the town for just good, comforting food.

"Your birthday's coming up. I'm thinking about a party here with a few of our friends. Think you can handle it?"

"As long as you don't invite half the town," Mark answered.

"I promise, it won't be your whole patient load and the only four-footed guests will be the ones that live here."

"OK, call the office tomorrow and make sure that Kate gets it on my schedule. I'm not good at remembering such things, but my staff keeps me in line."

"Don't worry, I'll remind you too."

Our conversation then wandered around happenings in town.

"Ready for malasadas?" Mark asked.

"I hope that's singular for each of us?"

"Well, she sent half a dozen, but I'm sure some could be saved for tomorrow."

"OK, pick out the smallest one for me and only put one scoop of ice cream on it."

Mark got our dessert ready while I cleaned off the table and put the dishes in the dishwasher.

"Let's go to the living room," I said as I picked up my bowl and headed for the couch again. This time I had to shove Sable out of the way in order to sit in my favorite corner. She gave me a dirty look as only a Siamese cat can and moved over to curl up next to Mark.

"You're very much out of favor," he said with a chuckle.

"She'll survive. I'll bet she'll be on my bed before I'm totally asleep."

"Won't take that bet."

"I wonder if Kelmen ever cared for his aunt." I broke the comfortable silence that we'd settled into. "Or was it always a charade to get her money?"

"I don't think we'll ever know for sure. I'll be interested to know if the money problems came from his gambling. I am willing to bet that we're correct on that count."

"Now I won't take that bet," I said.

"Well, we need to finish cleaning up your kitchen and I need to go toward home."

"You're probably correct on that, although it is sure comfortable here." But saying that, I got up and picked up my dish and Mark's. "Don't worry about any cleanup. There isn't much."

We moved to the back porch and I saw two white shadows start across the field toward us. The dogs had obviously taken advantage of Mark being with me to check out their territory before we settled in for the night.

"Hey," Mark said as they both jumped up on the porch at the same time. He knelt down to give them both a good scratch and a hug. I took advantage of that to get leashes on both of them so Mark could open the outside gate when he left.

"You take care of your mom, you hear?" he said as he got up and to me, "I'll call you in the morning but not too early. Probably just before I go into surgery."

"OK, but I'll be fine. The bad guy's behind bars."

"I know, but..." He reached over and pulled me in for a hug and a gentle kiss. Then he kissed me again with just a little more force. "God, you had me scared for a bit."

"All's OK thanks to you and Falcor. Now off with you so we can all get some sleep."

He gave me one more hug and walked out to his van. He gave one beep on his horn after he'd gotten through the gate, shut it, and turned onto the road. I waved although I wasn't sure he could still see me.

"Come on, monsters, it's time for us to clean up and go to bed."

Chapter 23

I watched as one more vehicle drove in and once more my dogs hailed the newcomer with greetings. Although the tone of these was slightly different because they knew this truck. It was Sean's. It was a gorgeous late spring afternoon and our friends had gathered to celebrate Mark's birthday.

"Glad you made it, little brother, Jeevana has been watching for you even though I'm sure she'd deny it."

"We'd planned on coming together, but I had to do a last-minute run to check out a possible burglary. Turned out to be an overzealous neighbor, but I'd rather have them be overzealous than never seeing anything. Now point me to the food before the locusts who arrived ahead of me eat it all up."

I laughed. "Most of it's set up on the side porch. Mark and Jonathon are at the barbecue, and I don't think you need to worry about some being left for you."

I followed him around the porch to the side of the house

where almost everyone was gathered. However, I noticed that a few had moved around to the front to take advantage of the old-fashioned swing. Some were sitting on the steps and all seemed to be having a good time.

I looked out over the garden and took in the late spring beauty. The rhododendrons and azaleas were in full bloom where they formed a hedge along the fence at the perimeter of the yard. The dogwoods were in bloom and the willow's graceful branches were dancing in the gentle wind. The daffodils and tulips still had a bloom here and there in shadier, cooler areas where they'd come up late, and the pansies were looking great. Other bushes and flowering plants would take the place of these as the summer progressed. I never tired of the beauty that greeted me from the garden sides of my house. I couldn't imagine living anyplace else. This was home.

"How's the cooking going?" I walked over to stand next to Mark as Jonathon turned a couple of steaks over.

"Just great. Want me to put one of these on a plate for you?"

"Not yet. I still need to do a little mingling and make sure everyone is taken care of. Save a few of the ribs for me. That's what I really want."

"Will do."

I wandered over to where David Swanson was talking to his mother.

"You two found enough to eat and drink?"

"You've got to be kidding. I may never eat again," David responded.

"Want to bet? I've heard that before," his mother said with a laugh.

"Do either of you know how Sheila's doing?" I asked.

"The will is moving through probate without any problems," David said.

"Joseba didn't contest it?"

"He made noises about it, but when his attorney got a look at the will, he advised Joseba to just drop it. I guess he listened to the attorney."

"And she's back at the ranch and settling in nicely," Dorothy chimed in. "Since it's just Sheila, who's easy to get along with, the neighbors have been stepping up to help her out until she can get totally on her feet. Plus her mother is standing guard to make sure that she doesn't work too hard and that people don't overtire her."

"Sounds like I can contact her now about that lamb I'm interested in."

"I'm sure any sales would be appreciated. I'd guess that money is tight until all the inheritance stuff is settled."

"OK, I'll give her a call this week."

"Give who a call?" Walter walked up to join us.

"Sheila. I'm hoping to buy one of her lambs. Now that we have you cornered, what else did you and Jonathon learn about Kelmen's motives?"

"It was pretty much what you'd put together. He had gambling debts that he couldn't pay. He needed money fast. And of course, now he won't get any of it. He can't gain from his crime so the insurance money will go to the estate and thus to Sheila. You should hear him on that subject. Let's just say that his language is not fit for anyone's ears."

"Did you find out whom he owed the money to?"

"We did, and his help in that area may well keep the prosecutor from going after the death penalty. He led us to a gambling club that we didn't know existed. It was in Tacoma and the local police there have pulled in almost all of the ringleaders. One has slipped through their fingers, but he seems to be a lesser player. One of them was putting a great deal of pressure on Kelmen to pay what he owed. Enough pressure to have Kelmen petrified and to trigger his actions."

"That's good news. Closing down one of those operations is always a plus for the communities. By the way, where's Mary? I'd hoped to see her today." Mary was Walter's wife and a member of the Thursday knitting group that met at my shop each week.

"She ended up being called in to the hospital." Mary was an RN in the emergency room at St. Peter Hospital. "They came up short for the swing shift today. She was not happy about it. She was really looking forward to this and had especially asked for today off."

"Well, take a plate home for her and let her know that we missed her."

"I'll do that."

"There you are." Mark walked up beside me. "It's time for you to sit and eat. I have our ribs on plates. Now you just have to add to it."

"Guess I have my marching orders, gang."

He led me over to the food tables and handed me a plate with way more ribs than I could possibly eat. "And I'm supposed to get around these and eat anything else?"

He grinned. "Here, give me what you don't want. I put the ribs for both of us on your plate just to see what kind of rise I'd get."

I laughed and moved most of the ribs to his plate. Then we started down the table to add to it. I'd provided the meat for the party, but our friends, including Sally, had brought everything else potluck style. The table was laden with good food of all types and kinds. It was hard to make choices, but soon my plate was full and I had a glass of wine in my hand. Mark and I moved to a table in the garden to sit with Ellen and Jonathon.

"Who's manning the barbecue?"

"Sean took over. Said that he'd just eat too much if he didn't have a job to do, and he had good company. Jeevana was sticking quite close to his side and holding his beer for him."

"I think my little brother has done very well this time around. I couldn't be more happy for them."

"I talked to Sheila yesterday," Ellen said. "She says to come by anytime and pick out the lamb you want. Her gift for all that you did for her and for Catalin."

"But I don't want a gift. She needs the money for the lamb."

"She'll do OK, I bought five from her and she says that the bank accounts turned out to still be in joint tenancy. She doesn't have to wait for probate to get her hands on those."

"I think that says that Catalin really didn't want her gone. She was looking for a way to get Sheila back home. It is so tragic that Kelmen's greed ended all possibility of it happening."

"I think so too, and it lets Sheila know that in spite of what she said, Catalin still loved her. It will hurt for quite awhile, as you know from your experience, but she's a strong woman and she'll find a life for herself again."

"Yes she will," I said. "I know. I have." I gave Mark's hand a squeeze under the table.

At that moment, I heard a guitar start on the porch and then the strains of "Happy Birthday" came across the lawn as Sally walked up to our table with a small cake covered with candles in her hands. She set it in front of Mark.

"Make a wish."

Mark gave me a long look, shut his eyes, opened them again, and with a huge breath blew out all the candles. I knew what he was wishing, I just didn't know if I was ready for it. Thank goodness he wasn't pushing me. He was letting me get there in my own time.

Everyone applauded. "That one is for you at this table, and Elizabeth will be over in just a minute with plates and ice cream. For everyone else, there are two huge cakes over on the table on the front porch. I want to take none home so eat hearty here and take seconds home for yourself and family."

"And," Leslie chimed in, "we give you ten minutes to eat cake and then you must come open your presents. I can't wait to see what you got."

I had a feeling from the devilish look in her eyes that there would be some gag gifts in amongst the others. I wondered whom she'd been plotting with.

Elizabeth brought our plates and ice cream and joined us along with David for cake.

"Happy birthday," David said and lifted his glass in a toast. We all followed suit and the cake was soon devoured amidst laughter and good companionship.

As Mark and I headed up to the porch once again so he could open his presents, I noticed that Ellen and Sally were marshaling people to start cleaning up. I thought about going over to help and then decided to let them do it. It was what they wanted to do anyway. Leslie had a great time handing Mark his gifts and making sure that the gag gifts were intermixed with the serious ones. He was soon wearing silly hats and holding up raucous tee shirts while thanking people for things like a gift card for gasoline which could be put to excellent use. As a large animal vet, he put a lot of miles on his van. I had given him my gift of a handknit sweater from handspun yarn earlier in the day. The yarn contained not only hair from Denali and

Falcor but also from Mark's golden, Ben. It had taken a bit of subterfuge to gather Ben's hair without Mark noticing, but I'd had help from his staff at the clinic. If Mark wondered why they were so delighted to brush Ben, he'd had the good sense not to comment.

As we reached the end of the presents, a couple of guitars came out and then a ukulele. Soon people were singing songs from near and far that someone in the group loved. The melodies wafted over my fields, and off in the distance as the sun started to go down, I heard the coyotes add their voices to the chorus.

"OK, gang," I heard Ellen's voice, "time to finish clearing up and get ourselves out of here."

I laughed. In many ways, my friend was the most disorganized of people, but when needed, she could move in and take charge with the best of them. Someone on a guitar started another round of "Happy Birthday" and people started gathering up their things and moving toward their cars.

Mark and I stood on the back porch and watched the last of them leave. It had been a wonderful day filled with love, laughter and good friends. As Mark walked out to shut the outside gate and let the dogs loose to join us, I thought that maybe tonight, just maybe, we wouldn't open the outside gate again.